The Patriot Joe Morton

The Patriot Joe Morton

Michael DeVault

Published 2014 by Creativia

Book design by Creativia (www.creativia.org)

Cover art by Cover Mint

patriot (pā'trē–ət)
n. one who loves, supports and defends one's country
The American Heritage Dictionary

September: Casey Morton

Chapter One

Joe Morton was never considered a stable man. He had never lashed out, was not taken to fighting in bars. In fact, no one could remember his ever going into a bar. But he wasn't what the good people of Cranston considered normal. If you were to put any of the twelve hundred or so citizens of the small east Texas town on the spot, you would arrive at some variation of "Joe simply doesn't do things the way people expect."

He didn't own a tractor, opting instead to pay the Carmichael boy a few dollars to run the bush hog over the eighty acres he had inherited from his great aunt. Every Sunday, he occupied the same pew at Cranston First Baptist and, like the rest of the men, refrained from speaking his amens, though he would nod at the appropriate moments. And every morning, Joe arrived for breakfast at the Truck Stop Café around nine, where from table seven, the booth against the window, he read The Cranston Sun and drank three cups of coffee before shuffling off to start his day–though what he did each day, no one could say for sure.

There were a lot of things no one could say for sure about Joe Morton. That was a problem for the people who lived in the town he had called home for the last forty years. So the good people of Cranston had always approached him with a measure of caution, a caution of which for the most part, they were never quite sure of the cause. They kept their concerns about Joe's tenuous mental state in check with a healthy dose of "just don't think about it" until, one Tuesday in September, the leather strip of bells went clattering against the glass door of the Truck Stop Café.

In those days, strangers so rarely came into the Truck Stop Café that Doris Greely, the morning waitress, didn't immediately know how she should react. She exchanged a quick glance with Harlan, her lone customer, before finally rising to greet the young man. For his part, the stranger stood in the doorway, patiently knocking a spot of dust from his blue suit and arranging a matching blue tie neatly beneath his lapels. It wasn't until the staccato beats of his shoes resonated against the tile that Doris looked down and recognized the patent leather shoes of an Air Force man.

"Well howdy, son," she said. "You must be up from the base?"

"Yes, ma'am. You wouldn't happen to know how to get to Macomb Road, would you?" He removed a small notebook from his inside breast pocket and double-checked the address, adding a self-affirming nod. "Yes. Macomb Road."

Later, Harlan and Doris would remember this event in excruciating detail. They would recall the manner in which the officer tilted his head just so to one side. Harlan would recite how, sitting with his back against the wall–as he always did–the small cross on the man's chaplain insignia reflected into Harlan's eyes. Doris would recount the softness of his hands and the peculiar accent she couldn't quite place, perhaps upstate Ohio, as it was one of the many places she had never visited. They would repeat these and a hundred other trivial details to the news crews, to reporters, and to tourists so eager to devour any detail of the story. At that moment though, Harlan and Doris had only one concern. It was Harlan who gave it voice.

"What you want with Joe Morton?"

"I'm sorry, sir. It's a personal matter," the officer replied.

Harlan waved a dismissive hand at him. "Well, son, we ain't got much time for personal matters around here."

Doris shot Harlan a biting look before turning back to the officer. "It's about his boy, ain't it?"

When the officer hesitated, Doris rested a hand on his shoulder. "It's okay, son. You don't have to tell us."

Harlan's head dropped, and his shoulders slumped. After a moment or two in silence, he lifted his head. "Head out the highway and take a left at the old feed mill–"

Doris interrupted. "Let me just draw you a map, son."

A few minutes later, she watched him cross the parking lot of the Truck Stop Café to the waiting Ford Taurus, take his seat behind the wheel, and momentarily confer with two other uniformed men in the car before driving out Highway 7. By the time she returned to the corner booth, Harlan was staring silently into his lap. For the next ten minutes or so, while the Air Force chaplain made his way out to Macomb Road, they alone would carry the burden of knowing the war had claimed one of Cranston's own.

While Harlan plucked imaginary lint from the black felt of his cowboy hat, Doris compulsively checked her makeup and tried to smooth her red hair tighter into the bun at the back of her head. She was about to start polishing the flatware when she heard Harlan's cup rattle against his saucer and she looked up.

"How about a refill, Doll?"

She shook her head. "Pot's gone cold. Besides, I think it's about time you headed home. Something tells me this is going to be a long week."

Chapter Two

For twenty years, whenever Doris arrived to open the Truck Stop Café, she had been greeted by the same empty parking lot. The rows of big rigs that used to idle in the parking lot belonged to a time before Doris had gone to work for Jimmy, before Harlan's daddy had succeeded in getting the Interstate to forego a route through Cranston, which had forced the closure of the Cranston Truck Stop and left as the only reminders an empty slab that used to be the station and a spotless, gleaming diner.

Yet on the morning after they learned of Casey Morton's death, Doris pulled into the parking lot shortly before dawn and was dismayed to find Harlan's black Chevy Silverado idling near the front door. It was the kind of development that made Doris question her decision to forego a domestic life in exchange for independence. For a moment, she considered returning home and calling in sick, but Harlan had already seen her headlights and was making his way towards the door.

Despite her misgivings about Harlan, his tenacity impressed her. That distinctive limp, the one lingering disability of a twenty-foot fall from an oil platform, rarely slowed him down.

She checked her makeup in the rearview mirror and took an extra few seconds to brush a stubborn tangle out of her hair. In the glow of the car, her hair still looked soft and red. None of the gray at her temples was visible, and in that place lit only by the dome light, it was easy to pretend she had not aged much in the last few years.

Harlan was sitting on the bench near the door when she finally made it to the front of the café. He was staring out across the pastures towards the horizon, to where a band of low clouds glinted with the first golden hints of dawn. Doris held the door open and gestured for him to enter.

"Coffee won't make itself, Harlan."

He didn't budge. "That's okay. Think I'll sit out here for a few and watch the sunrise. Looks to be pretty, don't it?"

"Suit yourself," she said, but she lingered. Instead of going inside, she let the glass door close and sat down beside him. "I don't think I've ever seen you here this early."

"We've got a lot of plans to make, now, don't we?"

She eyed him, at once curious and confused. "What plans?"

"The Morton boy. We got a hero coming home. That requires planning."

Doris momentarily considered arguing with him. She didn't know Joe Morton any better than anyone else in Cranston, but she knew he was a private man who might not take to the attention a Harlan Cotton production would bring to his quiet existence. But Doris knew stubborn, and she had long ago given up confronting futility. Harlan decreed the boy's memorial service would be a town event. That was the way it was going to be. No amount of persuasion would change that. So Doris did the only thing she could to combat her dread of the day that was about to unfold. She sat in silence and watched the sun rise.

They were still sitting there when Ted and Margie Bartley pulled in.

"Morning Doris," they said in unison.

"Y'all aren't usually here on a weekday."

"Thought we'd change it up a bit," Margie said. "I've been telling Ted for ages we're getting predictable."

Doris just nodded, aware of the real reason they were there on a Wednesday. She smoothed her apron flat as she stood and opened the door. While Ted and Margie settled into their booth, she slipped into the back room, past Jimmy in the kitchen and into the cubby behind the walk-in freezer. She fished through her apron until she found the hard edges of her cell phone, removed it, and dialed Carly Machen.

Doris counted the rings, judging by each additional ring just how deeply unconscious her night waitress was. Finally, after seven rings, a groggy Carly picked up the phone.

"Hello?" came the feeble voice from the other end.

"Carly, I need you," Doris said. She didn't bother masking the pleading in her voice and knew what it would take to get a twenty-two year old out of bed before eight a.m. "I'll take your shift tonight and tomorrow night. And we'll split tips sixty-forty."

"What? What's going on?"

"Your Uncle Harlan's called the whole damned town to the café to plan the Morton boy's memorial service," Doris said without thinking. It took her a moment to place Carly's silence into the proper perspective of four years of a schoolgirl romance followed by a ring and a promise of marriage after what had promised to be a short deployment in a short war. Though they both worked at the Truck Stop Café, the two were on different shifts. So Doris knew Carly only peripherally and, in any other situation, neglecting to remember the ins and outs of a coworker's love life would be at best a regrettable oversight. Now, though, Doris felt an emptiness that opened into the pit of her stomach. In all her haste, Doris had forgotten that Carly was Casey Morton's fiancé.

"Oh baby doll! I am so sorry," Doris said.

She could hear the unmistakable, muffled sounds of the girl crying into her pillow. Doris pictured Carly's jet black locks spilling over her face, her mouth open and dried tears streaking her cheeks. Doris wished she had remembered Carly and Casey before picking up the phone. She wished she could be there, in Carly's bedroom, cradling the girl through her grief. But more than anything, Doris wished she could bring Casey Morton back for Carly.

When at last she heard her coworker uncup her hand from the receiver, Doris tried again to comfort her. "Carly baby, I am so sorry. I just didn't think–"

"It's okay," Carly said. "I'll be there in a few minutes."

"No, you stay home. You don't have to come in. As a matter of fact, take the week off. I'll cover your–"

"No, I said I'll be there in a few minutes," Carly replied. Doris knew from the girl's insistent, almost defiant tone that arguing with her would be as fruitless as arguing with Harlan.

"Besides," Carly added, a tone of finality in her voice, "maybe I don't need to be alone right now. So I'll see you in twenty minutes."

The phone went dead before Doris could reply. She dropped it back into her apron pocket, leaned absently against the side of the walk-in, and succeeded in fighting back her own wave of tears. When she returned to the dining room, the number of customers had grown exponentially. In Doris's absence, Margie had donned an apron and was filling coffee cups.

"Hope you don't mind the help," she said with a smile.

Doris didn't protest, opting instead to listen in on the state of affairs. There would be a small memorial service at the town square. Harlan had already arranged to bring the band from Cranston High to provide the appropriate musical atmosphere. Johnston Metalworks would cut and install an additional half dozen flagpoles to line the sidewalk opposite the half dozen they placed at the nine-eleven commemoration a few years back.

"It'll make for nice effect leading up to the band stand, you know–from the south approach," Greg Johnston said, glancing around the room to gauge everyone's approval.

Doris saw Carly's Nissan pull into the parking lot and decided now was the time to speak up. "Guys, we need to table this discussion for a few minutes. Carly's here."

Doris immediately regretted saying anything, as every person in the Truck Stop Café fell silent and turned to watch the door. About halfway through the parking lot, Carly stopped, hesitated for a moment as she saw two dozen sets of eyes staring at her. She walked through the diner, to the register, and picked up a ticket book before turning to face them.

"Relax, everyone. I'm fine, really. I'm fine."

Doris slid an arm around Carly, gently squeezing her waist. She felt the light brush of fingertips before Carly pulled away and started directly for Harlan's table. Doris couldn't help but smile to herself at the girl's strength and, in that space of a few seconds, Doris knew futility found no home in Carly Machen.

Somewhere over the course of serving breakfast, Doris caught Carly's infectious resilience and found the fortitude to carry through the morning. Moving about the restaurant with a coffee pot, Doris picked up quiet snippets of recollections of this poem or that song. When Margie suggested her church choir could sing "The Battle Hymn of the Republic," she smiled. She dropped off another plate of bacon on Harlan's table and listened for a moment about a twenty-one gun salute–which Harlan assured the men the Air Force would provide.

Each time a sense of unease began to creep up her spine, she returned behind the counter and polished flatware for a moment or two. It was a simple act and one she often retreated to in anxious moments. The action of the soft cloth gliding over the smooth bowl of a spoon soothed her nerves. By the time the first lunch patrons arrived, Doris had lost the need to polish silverware altogether and deemed her initial apprehension misplaced. The people of Cranston understood more about Joe Morton than she thought. This memorial would be a celebration of Casey Morton's life and service, sober and appropriate.

While Doris was clearing away the last of the breakfast dishes and Carly was busy putting out the lunch menus, the Franklin twins arrived with their own offering for the service.

"We're volunteering our horses and the wagon. You know, to pull the coffin from the square to the cemetery," the first Franklin brother said.

Harlan nodded thoughtfully at the suggestion, rubbed his chin, and smiled. "That's mighty charitable of you, Jerry."

Ted Bartley cleared his throat. "If we're going to have a processional, someone needs to get Shep to sign off on it."

"Don't you worry about Shep," Harlan said. "I'll handle the mayor."

He polished off the last dregs of coffee in his cup and smiled. "Well, boys, looks like we're going to have a parade."

Chapter Three

Despite the creeping tingles in his left foot, Harlan was doing his best not to move. The vinyl cushion belched every time he adjusted his weight, and he was determined to spare himself the embarrassment of the young nurse's assuming his stomach was the culprit.

She smiled at him as she fastened the blood pressure cuff around his arm. "How was the trip down, Mr. Cotton?"

"Same as always. Long and boring," he said.

The truth was, though, Harlan had been thankful for the drive. The two hours from Cranston to Waco always gave him time to clear his head and order his thoughts. He had awakened before dawn, his mind filled with a jumble of minutiae for the Morton boy's service. By the time he arrived at the V.A., he had successfully ordered all the problems into manageable logistical categories.

The nurse removed the cuff and jotted the measurements onto the chart. He tried to read the numbers as she recorded them, but gave up. "So how'd I do?"

"Great," she said with a smile. "As always. One-twenty over eighty. Doctor will be in in a few."

She left the folder on the table and closed the door behind her. Harlan shifted his weight and sent a rush of blood to his aching foot. Someone had hung a poster outlining the human skeletal system on the back of the door, the kind of poster Harlan assumed medical types hung in order to make the room appear more medical. He had been to the V.A. so many times in the past year and a half, he began keeping track of which room he had been in by the posters. He saw similar maps of the nervous system, the vascular system and the digestive system, and not once did any medical person refer to the posters for explanation. The one time such illustrations would have been constructive, the doctor deferred instead to a bad photocopy to show him where the prostate was and the functions it provided.

The door opened and the doctor entered in silence. He reviewed Harlan's chart and jotted a few notes before looking up and removing his glasses. "Good morning, Mr. Cotton. How's life in Cranston?"

"More of the same, I suppose," he said. The doctor rested the stethoscope against his chest and he inhaled deeply.

"So any problems?"

"No, not really. We have a funeral day after tomorrow for a boy killed in Iraq, but that's–"

"I meant with your health?"

Harlan nodded. "No, nothing to speak of."

The doctor made a few more notes in the chart and flipped the page. As he read in silence, Harlan tried to read some significance in the man's expression but saw none. At last, the doctor closed the chart.

"So. All your labs look good. Normal. Blood pressure's solid. Other than the prostate, you're a picture of health. Especially for a man in his late sixties."

"And the cancer?"

"Well, like I told you. You'll always have cancer, unless we remove the prostate–"

"I don't want that."

"Right. So we're going to continue brachytherapy every year and checkups every six months. And we'll keep watch on your

P.S.A. levels for any changes. I'd also like to rescan your prostate on your next visit, just to make sure."

Harlan stood and began pulling on his trousers. "You got anything else I need to know?"

The doctor shook his head. "No, Harlan. But I see your billing address listed as a post office box? Still haven't told your wife?"

Harlan shook his head. "Ain't planning to, neither."

With a sigh, the doctor signed the chart. "I wish you didn't think you have to go through this alone, Harlan. It can be helpful to have someone to discuss things with, someone who knows what you're going through."

"That's what I got you for."

"That's not what I meant. I mean–"

"I know what you mean, and, no thank you. She don't know. She don't need to know."

The doctor shrugged. "Fine. It's your marriage. You're retired, Colonel. I can't order you to tell her."

"That's right, you can't. And even if I wasn't retired, Lieutenant Colonel–"

The doctor laughed. "Okay. Okay. You win. Just think about it? And make sure to come in for your labs in a few weeks. Don't skip it this time."

Harlan shook the doctor's hand. "Doc, it's not that I don't think she can handle it or anything. It's just–"

"I understand. I don't agree and I don't like it, but I do understand." The doctor tossed Harlan's chart onto the table and leaned back against the wall as his patient buttoned his shirt. "So tell me about this kid. The one who died?"

"Dad's from Cranston. He was dating Carly. My niece? The kid, not the dad. She's real busted up about it, but she's holding it together. Whole town's getting together for the memorial service at the end of the week."

The doctor smiled. "That's nice."

"It's going to be big. You should come down and see it."

"Nah, I've seen enough military funerals in my day. I'd just as soon not. But give my respects to his father."

Harlan nodded. He knew he wouldn't mention the visit to Joe, and the doctor didn't expect him to. It was just the kind of thing you said to a man.

They said their goodbyes and the doctor left Harlan with a handful of prescription slips for the pharmacy. When Harlan smiled at the nurse as he passed, she winked. As the doors to the V.A. closed behind him, Harlan felt a sense of relief. Another visit down, another good report. He climbed into his Silverado and, turning the key in the ignition, he paused and said a quick prayer of thanks.

"Amen," he said aloud and fired up the truck.

Chapter Four

Joe didn't return to the Truck Stop Café for three days and, for this, Doris was thankful. She understood he needed time to heal. Plus, she was unsure he would have been able to handle the onslaught of people that Harlan had assembled in those first couple of mornings. By the third day, though, talk had died down and was, for the most part, turning away from Casey Morton's memorial and to discussions of hunting lease rates for the fall and which road the aldermen would resurface first when the Legislature finally signed off on the state highway bill.

Life was slowly getting back to normal and Doris moved from table to table, topping off coffee cups and chatting with the truckers and, when they weren't alone, their companions. So busy was she that Doris could almost forget the war, Casey's homecoming and even the emptiness at table seven. Despite a full house, Joe's table had remained vacant throughout the mornings, as if the customers were anticipating his arrival any moment.

Doris had to admit she, too, was antsy. Dropping off an order at Ted and Margie's booth, she decided she would slip out to Macomb Road after her shift ended and take him a nice ham, or at least a banana crème pie. Those plans were dashed midway through breakfast when Joe turned up. And not much about him had changed.

At first, no one seemed to notice him taking his seat in the booth against the window. Harlan and the boys continued debating whether ducks or deer would be where the money was this season. Ted and Margie didn't bother looking up from their coffee and newspapers. Even Doris hadn't heard the clatter of doorbells when he came in. She had no idea how long he had been waiting when she finally noticed him sitting there, hands folded on the table, coffee cup turned upright on the saucer.

She scrambled over with the pot. "Didn't hear you come in, Joe. You want breakfast?"

He shrugged, then nodded.

"I'll fix you up, baby."

Doris rushed away from the table, scribbling an order for two eggs over easy, bacon, sausage and toast. As an afterthought, she jotted "on the house" across the bottom of the ticket before ringing the bell in the window. Jimmy took the ticket and hung it on the first clip.

"Good to see him back," he said.

When Doris returned to table seven a few minutes later with a second cup of coffee, she couldn't get to the table. Harlan and the boys were crammed into the booth, pressing in on Joe as Harlan outlined the town's plans for Casey's funeral.

"And then we'll turn at Fourth Street before heading up to Memorial Park for the concert and flag raising," Harlan said. "So what do you think?"

Joe was again staring across the parking lot, wordless and unmoving. Harlan batted him on the shoulder.

"Joe, you alright, buddy?"

Joe's nod was anything but committal. "Sure, Harlan. Sounds real nice. But you really shouldn't go through all the hassle."

"Nonsense. The boy's a hero." Harlan took a long draw off his coffee cup and winced. "A bona fide hero, he is."

Margie leaned forward and rested her hand on his shoulder. "You got any family coming into town?"

Joe shrugged. "My wife's sister, maybe. But ain't heard from her yet. She was traveling."

"Well, when she gets to town, you just let us know. We've got a room at the motel waiting for her. No charge, understand?"

Joe protested. "I don't want to put you out. This all just sounds like a whole lot of trouble."

"Trouble? It wouldn't be no trouble, Joe," Margie said. "Ain't like we don't have rooms going spare every night."

"That's right," Ted added. "It's the least we can do."

Doris shoved past Margie and Ted and up to the table, pausing long enough to shoot a disapproving glance at Harlan. She slammed the saucer down so hard coffee sloshed out of the cup and onto the table. Elbowing Harlan aside, she placed a roll of silverware at Joe's right hand.

"Here you go, Joe. And I'm making a fresh pot."

"Thanks, Doris," he said without looking up from the deep pool of the cup.

Several seconds of uncomfortable silence descended over the table. The men showed no sign of budging of their own accord and Doris wasn't about to leave them hovering while Joe ate. With a clap, she began waving them out of the booth.

"Y'all leave Joe alone. He's just wanting peace and quiet, don't you think? Shoo!"

The morning cadre shuffled away mumbling. Doris tried to laugh it off, but it wasn't working. "I'm sorry about that, Joe. They don't mean harm."

He forced a smile. "I know, Doris. They just want to help, I guess."

She paused, with the full intent of providing him the solace she knew he so desperately needed, but when their eyes met, Doris realized she didn't know what she was going to say.

"I...Joe, I'm–"

"It's okay, Doris. You think I wasn't ready for this when Casey signed up?"

Doris could only understand his strength through the context of her own sudden and quite inexplicable frailty. Joe's eyes were full of pain and confusion and anger, yet they also held an understanding so profound she couldn't put words to it. Instead, she reached into her apron and handed him her handkerchief, which he used to blot a solitary tear from his cheek.

"Joe, I'm real sorry about your boy," she said, just as Jimmy rang the bell. With a wink, she smiled. "I'll get your breakfast, then get out of your hair."

Loading Joe's order onto her tray at the service window, Doris realized the ridiculous amount of food she had ordered. She struggled to make it down the narrow aisle to Joe's booth where, when she arrived, Joe's eyes went wide at the buffet she laid out before him. She left his table without a word, folding his check and dropping it into her apron.

Throughout the morning, as he munched his way through breakfast, Doris kept a watchful eye trained for any window that might spring open and allow her to engage Joe in conversation. But such an opportunity never presented itself, and sometime while she wasn't watching, Joe sneaked out of the Truck Stop Café, leaving behind the morning paper and a twenty tucked beneath his saucer. By eleven-thirty, the place was empty and Doris was left with only Jimmy and a sea of empty booths.

Chapter Five

Doris tried to force her eyes to focus through the darkness as her thoughts fumbled with her location. She was in her bed, as her fingertips recognized the hand stitching of her mother's quilt. The bed was in her bedroom. This she knew by the rattling heater register in the floor. That meant she was in Cranston, at home, in the same house in which she had spent her whole life.

But something was not right.

She leaned across the bed and reached for the lamp. As her weight shifted, so did the bed. The right side of the headboard dropped another two inches. Doris had to grip the mattress to save herself falling to the floor. She finally reached the lamp cord and bathed the room in a warm light. As her eyes adjusted, Doris tried to determine what was happening. One of the posts had sunk into a splintered hole through the hardwood floor, as if the floor had grown hungry in the night and decided her bed would make a good snack.

Easing a tentative foot to the floor, Doris slipped from the bed and checked the clock. It was a little after five a.m. She slipped downstairs through the dark, empty house and into the kitchen, where she plugged in the coffee pot before reaching for the phone. She lifted the receiver and was about to dial a number when it occurred to her she had no one to call, especially not an hour before sun-up on a Sunday.

Instead, she returned the phone to the cradle and flopped into a chair at the breakfast table. Doris had lived in the house her great grandfather had built for her entire life, alone since her mother had died when Doris was twenty. The house, which had decided to swallow her bed. There, in the dark breakfast nook, between the back door and the Frigidaire, Doris wondered if the house had not swallowed her as well. Across the kitchen, the percolator hissed and slurped and belched. Through the big bay window, she could just see the distant horizon and the first hints of light in the sky. This must be what Jonah felt like, looking out of the mouth of the whale, she thought.

The air conditioner kicked on and she shuddered at the first hints of air down her neck. The clock on the stove told her it was almost five-thirty. By now, she could call most anybody in town without waking them up. But she was still at a loss. The only man she knew well enough to ask for help was Harlan, and she wasn't about to call him.

The house groaned as a breeze whipped around the corners. It was a sound Doris had grown so used to in the last forty years she probably wouldn't have noticed it on any other morning. But this one was different. With a sigh, she reached for the phone again and dialed Harlan's number.

The phone rang twice before someone picked up.

"Hello?"

It was Noreen.

"I hate to call so early, but I need a man," Doris said.

Noreen chuckled. "Everything all right?"

"Yeah. Everything's fine. Just a little house problem."

"I don't know how you do it, taking care of that place all by yourself. Hold on, hon. Let me go get him."

Doris could hear Noreen calling for Harlan. Then, a gruff cough before he answered.

"Morning, Doll. Reenie says you've a problem with your house?"

"The damned thing's trying to eat me," she said. "I know it's early, but–"

"Don't you mind that. I'll be over faster than you can pour a cup."

She would have thanked him, or at least told him to take his time, but the line was dead before she had the chance. Doris calculated the time it would take Harlan to drive from his house to hers and added a safe two minutes for him to put on his boots and get his keys. She would have just enough time to throw on some clothes and pull her hair back.

True to form, Harlan was there just before six. Doris heard his Silverado in the gravel drive and was waiting at the kitchen door with a steaming cup of coffee.

"Morning, Doris."

She handed him the cup. "Harlan, thank you."

"Don't you mind that, I told you. What's up?"

"Maybe I just ought to show you," she said.

Doris led him upstairs to the bedroom she had occupied her whole life. He immediately pursed his lips upon seeing the bed.

"This ain't good," he said. As if he sensed her apprehension, he cleared his throat quickly. "Could just be dry rot, though. This Texas air ain't always nice to hard wood."

She watched as he got down on one knee and prodded at the broken boards with the tip of a pocketknife. The floorboards seemed to disintegrate each time the blade made contact. At last, the blade met some resistance. Harlan removed the blade from the boards, studying the tip.

"Shit. Come take a look."

She knelt beside him and looked down into the hole. "Harlan, you know I ain't got a clue what I'm looking at."

He pointed to the blade. "See them?"

The outstretched blade was coated with what looked like sawdust, which would make sense, given that Harlan had been hacking away at a wood floor. But before she could say anything, the sawdust moved.

"Is that…?"

"Yep. You gotta call a bug man," he said.

Doris's heart sank.

"Great. How much is this going to cost me?"

He shrugged. "You're on the second floor. Probably came up the outside wall. If you're lucky, they only got this bit of the floor and whatever path they came up."

"And if I'm not?"

He sighed and didn't answer. Instead, he stood. "You gotta call a bug man. Today."

"I don't have one."

"I'll send my boy over. But he's going to charge you extra–"

"And this ain't something I can buy at the feed store?"

"Doris, they're eating your house, Doll. You gotta call–"

"All right! All right. I'll call your bug man."

"Good," he said. He started for the door but stopped and looked again at the bed. "Maybe you'd better let me call him for you."

Doris nodded. "I'd appreciate that."

"And before you go spending any money on repairs, you let me see the bid."

"Okay. But–"

"Doris, there ain't a builder in Texas wouldn't take advantage–"

She laughed. "All right, already! Now you get on home before Noreen starts thinking things."

After he drove away, Doris opened her purse, removed her pocketbook and returned to the breakfast table. She had not balanced her checkbook for a couple of months and now seemed like a good time to do so.

Chapter Six

Frederick Gruber surveyed his wife's handiwork from the foot of the bed he had shared with her for more than fifty years. His suit lay, pressed and flat, on the white tufted bedspread, the black wool free of so much as a hint of lint. A freshly bleached and starched Oxford was folded neatly and resting atop his pillow with his blue tie draped across it. Cecilia had even taken the time to polish the pair of black Florsheim wingtips before tucking a pair of his favorite argyle socks inside.

He couldn't recall when she first began laying out his suit before each workday and he wasn't about to question the practice. In their fifty years of marriage, Frederick's wife had never once missed a speck of dust. The one time he brought up the ritual, she shrugged it off with the suggestion he not mistake it for subservience. In time, Frederick understood it was her part in the solemn work to which the town of Cranston had entrusted the Gruber family since 1933. Frederick checked his watch, saw he had a few minutes before the motorcade was supposed to arrive, and decided he could afford himself the luxury of a moment to ponder life–or at least his place in it.

Twenty minutes later he failed to hear the doorbell, and Cecilia discovered him sitting at her vanity, looking not at the mirror but instead at his hands, folded in his lap. He didn't register her presence until she touched him on the shoulder.

"Everything okay, darling?" she said.

He glanced up, his lips registering only the faintest hint of a smile. "Yes, dear. I was just thinking about something my father once said. He told me those in our line of work have a unique way of looking at life. I understand what he means now."

"Well, understand it while you're getting dressed. Joe's downstairs and the Sheriff will be here any minute with the motorcade."

Frederick nodded and rose to dress. He hesitated as his knee almost gave out, steadied himself on Cecilia's shoulder, and then smiled. "False alarm. Tell Joe I will be down in a moment."

She stretched to kiss him on the cheek before leaving him to dress in peace before the day's spectacle began.

For the first time that day, he allowed himself a moment of dread, of regret about the events that were about to unfold. When Joe's wife died more than a decade before, it was Frederick Gruber who coordinated the restrained memorial service attended by just a few intimate friends in the smaller of the two Gruber Family parlors. Today, sometime after one, Casey Morton's body would arrive by special flight at Tyler Pounds Regional Airport, where Joe Morton—and half of east Texas, it seemed—would meet him.

Almost nine days dead, and just now getting home, Frederick thought. And to come home to all of this.

"It's undignified," he heard himself say aloud. "Not their place."

"Our place," Cecilia corrected him from the door. "You live here, too."

"Yes, but I'm not a part of…that." He waved his hand in the air in the general direction of town.

"I know you're not, sweetheart, but you have to go for Joe. Now go do your job. Don't keep him waiting."

She patted his chest, stretched up to kiss his cheek before hurrying back downstairs. Frederick checked his hair in the mirror, straightened his tie, and, with a sigh, followed. Downstairs, he found Joe in a chair, hands folded neatly in his lap, staring into the small chapel across the foyer.

"Hello, Joe," Frederick said.

He nodded. "I figured I'd meet everybody over here, save them a trip out to the house."

"You should not have done that. I would have been–"

"I needed to. Everyone's already done so much," Joe said. He stood and extended a hand and, when Frederick took it, the grip was strong, steady and without any sense of the weakness Frederick had expected.

"Joe, do you have any questions about this morning?" he asked.

Joe shook his head. "No, everyone explained it to me pretty good."

"Okay, old friend. We can–"

"Fred, will I be able to see him?"

The Gruber family had been Cranston's sole funeral providers for three generations, ever since Frederick's grandfather had fled from Europe with the family. Though he was only an infant during the 1940s, Frederick had seen Korea and worked through Vietnam. He buried grandmothers and infants, but never had he so profoundly understood grief until that moment.

"Of course you can see him, Joe. No one will tell you otherwise."

Joe flinched when the doorbell rang and Frederick smiled. "I know just how you feel, old friend."

Sheriff Tolar was the first to enter the small foyer, flanked by the Mayor on one side and Harlan on the other. Frederick and Joe in turn shook each of their hands. With this cursory greeting, an uncomfortable hush descended and the five men were reduced to staring at their feet, waiting for someone to breach the silence.

Frederick exchanged a glance with Joe and then cleared his throat. "Gentlemen, should we?"

"Yes," said Harlan. "You ready, Joe? We got you a limousine."

Joe shook his head. "It's too much, Harlan. I don't need all this."

"You can't drive yourself," the sheriff said. "It'll relax you."

Joe heaved a sigh, but before he took another step, Frederick maneuvered between Joe and Harlan. "Joe, would you like to ride with me?"

"In the hearse?" Harlan scoffed.

"Yes, Mr. Cotton. In the hearse."

Joe looked at the hearse, then the limo. Without hesitation, Joe fell in behind Frederick. Frederick felt Harlan bristle as he walked past him, following Joe Morton to the car that would bring his son home for the last time.

Chapter Seven

Joe said nothing during the thirty-minute car ride to Tyler. At first, Frederick was worried about the silence and tried to make small talk to keep Joe's mind occupied. Though by the time the motorcade reached the airport, Frederick's mind had settled enough to remind him Joe was simply being Joe and the silence no longer was a concern.

He steered the hearse past the two TSA guards flanking the open gate and onto the tarmac, bringing the great car to a stop behind the sheriff's escort and the limousine carrying Harlan and the Mayor. They were in front of a large hangar. The giant rolling doors were open and waiting. Somewhere inside was Casey Morton. A young Air Force officer rushed forward to open the passenger door for Joe.

"Mr. Morton, sir," he said. Joe nodded as he exited the car and extended his hand to the man.

"Is it time for me to see my son now?"

Before the officer could reply, Harlan closed the distance between them and interrupted. "Joe, buddy, I don't know that's such a good idea."

He looked first to the sheriff then to Frederick, as if cuing them for support, but both men remained silent.

Joe shook his head. "No. I want to see my boy, Lieutenant."

Only Frederick understood Joe was now at the place of closure, that seeing Casey's body there in the hangar, in his casket, would confirm that his son was gone. Even though Harlan's concern was well intentioned and not altogether unjustified, Frederick knew there was no way the motorcade back to Cranston would leave before Joe had seen his son.

"Harlan, boys," Frederick said. "These military guys. They know what they're doing. It will be fine."

Throughout the exchange, Joe's eyes had never left the door leading into the small room off the hangar. Frederick rested his hand against the door but stopped before opening it. "Are you sure, Joe?"

Joe inhaled deeply. "Yeah, I think. Yeah."

Inside, Joe and Frederick were greeted by the same young officer who had met them in the hangar. He snapped to attention and saluted the men. Joe nodded his response and the young man remained at attention beside the coffin. Joe stepped forward and ran his fingers along the top of the coffin in an attempted to open it. When he failed, he turned to Frederick, a look of helplessness on his face. Without hesitation, Frederick stepped between Joe and the casket. Though the mechanism was not difficult, he took his time with it, in order to better position himself between a father and the corpse of his son. If need be, he would have an extra moment to prepare Joe for whatever lay waiting inside.

When the mechanism finally clicked, his assessment of the skill of military morticians was proven correct and he breathed a small sigh of relief. Casey's face and neck were free from any visible signs of the bomb blast that killed him. His hair, always shorn, was exactly as it had been on the day the boy had left for boot camp. To all appearances, Casey's body was pristine with the one exception of the dry and chipped fingernails of someone who has spent time in the desert.

Joe stepped up to the coffin, resting his hand atop Casey's head. "Thank you, Fred. Thank you."

Frederick moved to place his arm around Joe's shoulders, but hesitated before letting it fall limply to his side. Such gestures, movements that he had made a thousand times before, suddenly seemed weak and incapable of providing the support Joe needed in that moment. Frederick knew, in point of fact, that no words he could say would suffice. After all, he had never buried one of his own children. He moved to speak, but was surprised to hear not his own voice but the voice of Joe, who spoke first.

"It's hard to explain, Fred. I sent my boy out into the pasture on a dirt bike when he was nine. I knew it was dangerous, that something could happen to him. But I had faith that he would be okay, that God would take care of him. Then it was high school and football and the tackles and still, faith. God would protect him."

Joe stepped away from Casey's coffin and took a seat in a chair against the opposite wall. Frederick thought for a moment Joe might break down in tears. Instead, Joe offered him the seat beside him.

"He came home, so excited. When that recruiter came to the school. College, he said. He could go to any college he wants. And get to see the world, he told me."

Joe laughed. "I tried to tell him he could go to any college he wanted and see the world that way, but he wouldn't hear anything of it. No. The Air Force. That's what he wanted to do."

Joe's shoulders slumped, his head to the side, as if the weight of relived emotions had fallen on him yet again. Of course Frederick knew this story, knew every detail of Casey's enlistment, boot camp. His first deployment to Afghanistan, then a second tour after the invasion. And then off to Iraq. But years of experience had taught Frederick Gruber the greatest skill an undertaker can develop: silence. He realized as he listened to Joe narrate, that though he knew all the details, he had never before heard it told first hand.

" 'Son, why not wait? You have time. Carly and you could pick a school,' I told him. I had the money. They could have gone anywhere. And for a while it looked like they would. He graduated, spent the summer working in Dallas. Then it happened. He'd just come home the night before so we could spend a few days together. We were at breakfast together, at the Truck Stop, when Harlan came in and told Doris to turn on the T.V. because something had happened."

When Joe paused, Frederick looked up and saw the beginnings of tears in the corners of Joe's eyes. But still, he gave Joe silence he needed. Practice told the old German that Joe still wasn't finished.

"So Doris turns it on. And right there, on the screen, is New York. And we watched the second plane hit. I knew then, Fred. While everyone else was worried about terrorists and airplanes, I was worried about my son. Because I knew there was no stopping him. He signed the papers that day," Joe said.

The tears had stopped, and now, Joe was almost smiling.

"I was never more proud of him than that afternoon. But I knew, Fred, I just knew. God had kept him safe on that motorcycle and had kept him safe on the ball field. But something told me this was it. When he signed those papers I lost my boy."

Chapter Eight

During a two-decade tenure as mayor, John Shepard had seen hundreds of exhibits in the small foyer of the Cranston Town Hall. The space, roughly the size of Shep's dining room, had played host to quilting displays and bake sales. Once, for three whole days, the vestibule had been home to a blue-ribbon pigmy sow, inexplicably named Papa. None of it, however, compared to the presence of Senior Airman Casey Morton's flag-draped coffin.

At first, Shep was impressed by the sheer magnitude of the display. The casket took up surprisingly little space, even considering the portable stand Gruber Funeral Home had lent for the purpose. But the flowers! He had never seen so many carnation sprays and wreaths, each struggling to find a uniqueness in a wall of red, white and blue fluff. Along both sides of the foyer, at least three rows deep, flower baskets and broad-leafed tropicals fought for space along the walls. It was too easy to assume that the smallness of the space was simply overwhelmed by the sheer number of plants, but Shep knew otherwise. The lobby wasn't that small, and he had been there the previous day when the first delivery arrived. He and his secretary watched the lobby slowly fill with every imaginable botanical variation until, at last, the final delivery, before Casey's coffin arrived.

"Would it be okay if we block the entrance to your office for the night?" Gruber's delivery boy had asked. At the time, Shep hadn't given it a second thought.

But now, the morning of the boy's funeral, he was suddenly very regretful. The American Legion Post Commander had insisted all of the Cranston men wear their garrison caps to the service as a show of respect to their fallen comrade. Like everyone else in the Cranston post and, Shep suspected, around the nation, his hat was in the most logical place: next to the Lion's Club pen in the top drawer of his desk, ready to be worn to noon luncheons twice a month and returned immediately after.

Shep plotted the most accessible course through the flowers. If he moved two wreaths and a small elephant ear, he might be able to squeeze between the easeled picture of Casey and the American flag made out of dyed gladiolas. It would, however, require him to step over and around the potted silk ficus, the one plant that actually lived beside his door. All very doable, he told himself, especially if he wanted to avoid disturbing Casey Morton's coffin. But Shep wasn't as agile as he had expected to be. Instead of finding the secure footing of a wing-tip on polished tile, his toe came down in the mossy entanglement of the ficus. For the briefest of moments, Shep thought he was going to fall and had a vision of his secretary arriving an hour later and finding him splayed on the floor beside the boy's casket, dead from head trauma. Before his hand found the doorknob to steady himself, Shep had long enough to wonder if his death or Casey's funeral would be the top story in the paper the next morning.

But today was not to be his day.

Instead of a sudden and unexpected demise, Shep found himself propelled forward into his office. The door slammed firmly behind him. He rested back against it, the knob still grasped firmly in his hand and tried to get his heart to slow a bit. Before he could catch his breath, the phone began to ring.

At first, he ignored it. It was probably his wife, telling him to remember his hat or Harlan, demanding additional police officers to escort the cortege. His garrison cap was right where he had left it, in the top right hand drawer of his desk with his Bible and the Cranston town charter.

The phone stopped ringing. Must not have been important, he told himself.

Shep rolled the hat up, tucking it into his pants pocket before heading for the door. He checked his watch and saw he had almost an hour before the procession began and decided to review the waterworks grant the town council had just approved. Maybe a new water tank would come of it, or at least a new coat of paint on the old one.

The message light on his phone lit up. Shep wanted to ignore it, but the insistent red light blinked again and again until, finally, he succumbed to its demand that he reconnect to the world outside his sanctuary.

Shep sighed when he heard the familiar voice on the recording.

"Shep, Harlan. We got an issue down here at the bandstand. Want your help in the matter. Call me back," Harlan said.

The mayor returned the phone to the cradle with a sigh. Call him back? Why? He was three hundred yards away at the bandstand on the town square. Hell, Shep thought, why not just open the window and yell?

But he didn't.

Instead, he pushed his chair out, closed the folder on the waterworks grant, and started for the square and the bandstand and whatever crisis Harlan felt warranted a phone call at half past seven in the morning.

Traversing the town square, Shep began to get a sense of what lay in store for the town that morning. There were the new flags, hoisted to half-mast across from the old flags. A dozen identical red, white and blue standards flanked both sides of the broad walkway up to the bandstand. Along each side of the walk stood another four-dozen miniature facsimiles of the flags above, staked into the dirt on dowels. The banisters of the bandstand were decked in star-spangled bunting and a pulpit had been placed to the left of where the coffin would rest during the service. Three rows of folding chairs had been set out on the lawn and marked reserved for the dozen or so distinguished guests and, on the bandstand, four white pews had been brought down from First Baptist. Surveying the town square, Shep had to admit Harlan had outdone himself.

He looked around the bandstand and finally found Harlan, hunkered in a corner, fiddling with the microphones. He cleared his throat to make his presence known.

"So what's the crisis, Harlan?"

Harlan didn't look up from the tangle of wires. "You didn't have to come all the way down here, Shep."

"I was already here. No bother. What can I do you for?"

"Mary Jo Shively brought those," Harlan said. He nodded to a stack of papers lying on the pulpit. "Portraits, from her art class. Of Casey Morton."

"Well ain't that sweet," Shep said. He began leafing through the stack. Some of them showed a young man wearing a uniform. Several of them contained flags and fireworks. The last one even showed a soldier atop a tank. There were soldiers with brown hair and blue eyes in fatigues, soldiers wearing tee shirts emblazoned with ARMY in strong letters, and a soldier wearing a purple heart.

"Miss Shively wants them displayed next to the coffin," Harlan said. He let his words hang in the air, as if to import some meaning to them. Shep returned the drawings to the podium.

"I fail to see what a few schoolhouse drawings will take away from the service," Shep said. "Besides, I'm sure Joe will appreciate the gesture."

Harlan stood, at last satisfied with his handiwork on the sound system. He dusted his hands and eyed the mayor.

"Shep, we go way back."

"Yep, Harlan, we sure do."

"And I consider us friends," Harlan said.

"Then you won't need me to remind you that I'm the mayor and you're on city property. The drawings will make a fine addition to the service," Shep said, satisfied with the finality of his pronouncement.

In the distance, a bell tolled eight. Both men looked toward the horizon.

"Only an hour before the funeral, Harlan. Best get someone posting those pictures, don't you think?" Shep said. "As a matter of fact, Harlan, I'll do the honors. There's a stapler in my office."

Harlan was about to protest, but Shep raised a hand.

"No need to offer to do it yourself, Harlan. Consider it my contribution to the day," he said.

Walking away from the bandstand, Shep smiled to himself at the sudden burst of courage. Standing up to Harlan Cotton was something he should have done a long time ago. His stride increased, his step lightened and, for the first time in as long as he could remember, John Shepard felt like the mayor of Cranston.

Chapter Nine

When Doris first awoke on the morning of Casey's funeral, she had not intended on partaking of the services. Instead, she would do exactly as she had done every morning for the past twenty years. She would open the Truck Stop Café for breakfast, work through lunch, and go home around four–in spite of Harlan's insistence she would be "waiting on an empty café." Only after Doris saw the look on Carly's face when the girl learned Doris would not be there did she agree to attend.

"I don't think I'll be able to face this alone," Carly had said. Standing near the bandstand, awaiting the arrival of the casket, Doris came to fully appreciate Carly's instincts. Doris could only marvel at the scene.

Every inch of the Cranston town square had been draped in cloth of red, white and blue that seemed to radiate its own heat in the late-September sun. On every building hung at least one American flag, if not two or three. The parking lots along Main Street had been kept empty the night before by orange traffic cones, which had in turn been replaced shortly before dawn by bunting-draped police barricades borrowed from Dallas and Houston.

People crowded two deep along the bunting and the crowd grew deeper near the bandstand, where the service would be held. Behind the rows of seats marked "reserved," two groups of children were alternately playing tag or duck-duck-goose. Doris tried to focus on something, anything really, that didn't remind her of the farce in which they were all taking part but all she could think about was the poor Air Force honor guard.

Six uniform-clad airmen stood in two lines at unflinching attention, their rifles hoisted to one shoulder. Three more stood guard nearby, watching up the street. They were waiting for the arrival of the coffin and Doris could see beads of sweat forming on their cheeks and foreheads. Their hats seemed to provide little in the way of shade. Doris wanted to offer the boys a drink of water or a ride out of town, but knew the airmen and she had something in common. They were there not for the crowd, not even for Casey, but for Carly and Joe.

In the distance, Doris heard the clop-clop-clop of hooves on pavement and turned. The limbers and caissons had turned onto Main Street for its ceremonial trip to the bandstand. An honor guard of ROTC cadets up from College Station marched at the head of the procession in solemn, deliberate steps. Behind them came first Casey's flag-wrapped coffin and then, immediately behind the carriage, members of the Cranston town council, the Mayor and Harlan Cotton.

"Isn't everything just perfect?" said a voice over Doris's shoulder. She looked up to find Margie Bartley standing beside her. "Don't tell Mr. Johnson, but I think one of the new flag poles is crooked. Other than that, I mean. What do you think?"

"I think it's kind of ridiculous," Doris said.

Margie ignored her. "All of it is just so…patriotic! It makes you just want to go up and hug the Statue of Liberty."

"Yeah, that's what it makes you want to do," Doris said. She would have fled across the street to get away, but the cortege had arrived and the town fathers were supervising the process of assisting the six airmen in removing the coffin from the wagon.

Before Doris could retreat into the crowd, Margie leaned in to her and whispered, "What is the protocol?"

"What on earth are you talking about?" Doris said.

Margie nodded at the approaching funeral party, as if her meaning was apparent enough. When Doris did not immediately signal her understanding, Margie heaved a huge sigh.

"You know. With the coffin. I mean, should we bow or something?"

"Oh for the love of God, Margie. It's Casey Morton. Not the goddamned King of England. Protocol? I got your protocol, all right."

Doris noticed Carly tucked into a corner of the bandstand, alone. She started to leave, but Margie stopped her.

"What is your problem, Doris? We're all just trying to pay our respects."

"No, you're not, Margie. Paying your respects would have been going to a quiet graveside service, not turning this into a spectacle. Now can I go take care of Carly, or do you people not care about her feelings either?"

Margie fell silent, her eyes settling on the crying girl on the bandstand. She shook her head silently and prodded Doris on. Doris managed to mount the steps up the rear of the bandstand just as the airmen were setting the casket down. She slid into the chair beside Carly and rested her hand on the girl's shoulder. Carly turned with a start.

"Oh, it's you," Carly said. She entwined her fingers in Doris's, pulling her coworker closer to her. "I was afraid you were someone else."

As the town fathers all settled into their assigned seats, Carly did not let go of Doris's hand. Instead, she leaned over, dropping her head to one side and drawing her cheek along Doris's fingers.

"Carly, baby, you just hold on," Doris said. "It's almost over."

She felt Carly tense.

"You know what the hardest part is, Doris?"

"What's that, baby girl?"

Carly watched the airmen as they exited the bandstand. Just as Reverend Smith mounted the podium, Carly released Doris's fingers and patted the back of her hand. The girl's eyes followed her fiancé's coffin. Doris couldn't help but notice from her position Carly wasn't crying. Instead, her eyes were glassy, cold, the tearless eyes of a girl who had already done all the crying she could do. Carly turned to Doris and snorted.

"The hardest part is I got a letter yesterday from Iraq. Casey sent it. It said he'd just been told he was coming home at the end of the month," Carly said, looking again at Casey's coffin. "I guess he was right."

March: Carly Machen

Chapter Ten

If there were one thing Harlan liked more about life in Cranston than anything else, it was the relative ease of making everyday choices. Though he'd spent more time in Waco in the past year than in all the years before combined, Harlan still winced at the city's overwhelming barrage of alternatives touted from billboards on the highway and bulletin boards in the V.A. Back home, matters were simpler. Families going out to dinner went either to Mia's Pizza or Chow Yung's for Chinese. A working woman on a Tuesday morning off could always count on spending two hours for a wash, trim and roller set at Judy's on the Square, Cranston's only beauty shop. And a man in want of a new handle for his daddy's claw hammer went to Golson's Hardware.

"See, this one's got a bell face, so it's more forgiving if you miss," Golson said. He was attempting to show Harlan a new, composite-handled hammer with a bright, fluorescent yellow grip. When it became apparent to the old man Harlan wasn't paying attention, the old man nudged him.

"Just can't figure it out, Ernest."

"Hammers are a pretty straight-forward idea, Harlan."

He shook his head. "No, no, no. The Creedmore Building. What do you suppose old Joe's up to in there?"

He grew more frustrated when Golson ignored his query and said, "Maybe if you just tried to swing it once?"

Harlan turned to the man beside him and shook his head. "No. Something in hickory or ash."

If Ernest Golson wasn't convinced Harlan hadn't even seen the hammers he had spent the last twenty minutes showing him, that impression was confirmed by Harlan's gaze. His eyes had remained fixed on the plate glass window, or more precisely, on what lay directly across the street from Golson's Hardware. For the plate glass window and, by extension, the hardware store and everything in it lay in the shadow of the Creedmore Furniture building.

Harlan turned to Golson and took the hammer he was offering. "It's too light."

"Swing it once. Take a whack at something."

Harlan measured the weight in his hand, swung it a couple of times from the wrist, but the feel was all wrong. Hammers weren't supposed to be light and easy to wield. They needed weight and heft. Besides, Harlan wasn't concerned with the wall of hammers. Across the street, Joe Morton's truck hadn't moved for the better part of the day and Harlan was growing short of reasons to remain downtown anymore.

Six months with no Joe-related news had ended that morning with the revelation of Joe's purchase of the Creedmore Building. Since hearing that bit of gossip, Harlan had made two trips to the pharmacy, gotten a haircut and dropped by Shep's office unannounced. The broken hammer handle was the last excuse he could muster to remain near Town Square, and it happened to be the valid one. There was a hole in his fence and he needed a hammer to patch it.

Harlan nodded to the building across the street. "You ain't got a concern about what he's doing in there?"

Golson answered with a question of his own. "Never quite know with a man like Joe, do you? Besides, I don't much think it any of my concern."

Harlan placed the hammer back on the incorrect hook. "Unless he's opening a hardware store."

Golson laughed. "And buying his tools here? I don't much reckon."

"What sorts of tools?"

Golson shrugged. "I dunno. The guys said he came in yesterday and bought ten gallons of black paint and rollers and two sets of tin snips. Asked about arc welders."

Harlan tried to work out the details. Joe's behavior had become even more erratic in the months since Casey's funeral until he at last vanished from view altogether. The paint was easy enough; all the ground floor windows of the building had been painted black. There could be any number of uses for tin snips and a welding machine, but none of them made any sense. As Harlan surveyed the building once again, he grew even more uneasy and unsure of what he was expecting to find.

Aside from blacked out windows, Creedmore Furniture had not changed in its forty-year history as Cranston's only "modern" building. At three stories, it was the tallest building in downtown, bested in height only by the First Baptist steeple and the water tower. Its pale yellow brick and glass block second-floor windows did not fit in with the staid, red brick facades of Cranston's more classic downtown. Harry Creedmore had decided to build the store in the late 1950s when he learned from a friend in Austin that Cranston was on the proposed route for an interstate highway that was sure to "put Cranston on the map." It was the kind of tip from an old family friend upon which fortunes are made or lost. For Harry Creedmore, it was destined to be the latter.

A furniture store had always been his dream, so he sold their farm and began planning. Two years and three stories later, ground was broken on the new interstate, a hundred miles away in Waco, taking Harry Creedmore's furniture empire dreams with it. He closed the store and moved to Arizona before the first sofa made it to the showroom floor. To Harlan, the building represented a forgotten part of Cranston's history that he barely remembered from his adolescence, dredged up and made fresh again with the presence of an old pickup truck and freshly painted windows.

"Harlan, are you listening?" he heard Golson say.

The man was persistent in offering him another new hammer. "This one's a bit heavier. Twenty ounces. Fiberglass handle, with a nice curve for reciprocal action."

Harlan decided to humor Golson, even though he knew what it was he wanted to buy and would, in fact, buy. He mimicked swinging it a couple of times, then shook his head.

"Ernest, it's not that I don't appreciate your suggestions. There ain't a reason to rebuild the wheel. It's my hammer. I got it from my daddy, and he got it from his daddy, who used it to build the barn and the fence. The same fence I was mending when the handle split. I've already burned out the head and just need a new handle. Something in hickory or ash will do."

Golson sighed, rubbing his temple. "That's just it, Harlan. We don't sell just handles anymore. Everything's gone composite or fiberglass."

Before Harlan could respond, a man entered the store with a teenaged boy in tow. He was tall, too tall in fact, and had to stoop when he entered. Despite his deeply lined and weathered face, something in the man's bearing put Harlan off. He seemed too stiff, almost formal beneath the brim of a crisp fedora, from where his eyes traced a path among the shelves. His eyes, dark and foreign, seemed almost to consume the room.

When those same, dark eyes settled on Harlan and Ernest Golson, he smiled, set a rusting toolbox on the floor, and removed his hat.

"That is a very nice hammer, with a very nice reciprocal action," he said, his voice tinged with a heavy Latin accent. "But this one, with the bell head, is much better, especially for driving ten-penny nails through fence posts."

The man lifted the yellow-handled hammer Golson had first shown Harlan and offered it to him, handle first.

When Harlan did not move to accept the hammer from him, the man returned it to the shelf and straightened his posture.

"How'd you know–"

The man smiled.

"I noticed the lumber in the truck parked outside and made the connection. Please forgive the intrusion, gentlemen. I am Vítor Barros. This is my son, Téo," he said, pushing the boy forward slightly.

"Can you tell us where to find Mr. Joe Morton?"

Chapter Eleven

Whenever Harlan needed to turn things over in his head, he went out to the ranch. The familiarity of boyhood streams and summer campouts bred a certain comfort that usually gave Harlan the clarity he needed. When the V.A. doctors first told him of the cancer, he cleared the brush from the old corral while exploring the implications of the treatment options. In the months since the Morton boy's funeral, Harlan had spent a lot of time on the ranch but found little of the clarity he sought. Steering the Chevy down the dirt road bisecting his grandfather's eight hundred acres, Harlan wasn't hopeful.

The previous year notwithstanding, change wasn't something Harlan ever gave a lot of thought to in his sixty-six years. It wasn't that he had something against people who wanted things different than things were in Cranston. He appreciated the desire to see the world, but that was just the thing he didn't understand. The world was out there, waiting to be seen. There was no reason to bring it home to live.

And who was this Vítor Barros?

Harlan brought the Chevy to a stop under the shade of a live oak. He'd have to walk the last hundred feet to the back fence. Halfway down the hill, he realized he had forgotten the hammer and nails that had taken him to Golson's Hardware in the first place. Almost immediately, he regretted not loading up one of the horses and bringing it out. Nearing the truck, he could hear his cell phone ringing. He grumbled at the caller I.D. flashing his wife's name.

"Hello?"

"What time you gonna be home?" Noreen asked.

"Noreen, I'll be home when I get there," he said. Her tone wasn't demanding and Harlan immediately regretted taking it as such.

"Well, excuse me for interrupting your busy life, Mister."

"I'm sorry. The boys are all going over to Ted's to–"

"Put it off. Carly wants to have dinner with us."

Harlan remained silent. Anything he might say would just ignite a volatile situation. He also knew Noreen wouldn't give up until she got her way. He tried to judge by the angle of the sun in the tree how much good daylight he had before it became too dark to work.

"Harlan?" Noreen said. "You still there?"

For a second he almost didn't answer. She would assume the call had dropped and he could return home at his leisure. Doing so was a lie, though. So he sighed.

"Yeah. I'm still here."

"She said she's got a present for your birthday that she wants to give you before she goes out of town this weekend. And something about news."

"I'm not up for this tonight, honey."

"Up for what?"

"News ain't never good. It's Carly code for something we aren't going to like."

Noreen shushed him. "Don't you come down on her. Her boy's just come home in a box."

"Six months ago–"

"Like that's long enough to get over that kind of pain."

"Pain she could have avoided if you'd backed me up five years ago," he said too quickly.

"Casey was never good enough for your Carly," Noreen said.

Harlan fell silent again. It wasn't true. He always liked Casey who, despite his father's hermit streak, always behaved as any suitable young man should. His only objection to Carly's relationship with the boy came when Casey joined the Air Force. Harlan had lived through Vietnam and saw firsthand what war could do to a man. What Harlan had never said to his wife, what he fought against saying in that moment by listening to the breeze rustling through the leaves of the live oak, was the most painful of the truths. From the moment Casey Morton slipped that ring onto Carly's finger, there were worse outcomes for the girl than her boy coming home in a box.

"I'll be home in half an hour," Harlan said.

"Thank you," she said before hanging up.

Harlan tossed the phone onto the seat and climbed into the cab. For the entire ride home, Harlan tried to steer his mind away from pictures of those worse outcomes he had witnessed firsthand, the men coming home shell shocked or missing limbs or both.

His Army duty ended the day the first Marines went into Vietnam. He married Noreen the next month, in April, and spent the next two years volunteering in the makeshift convalescent ward at the V.A. During that time, he witnessed what became of men, barely more than boys really, reduced to a deathly silence punctuated by blasts of inexplicable anger. Sometimes, he regretted not re-upping himself and joining the fight. Most of the time, though, he could look down one of the halls and find a young girl not much younger than his Reenie and watch as she nursed her soldier through those bouts. In every one of them, the girls, he watched as they fought their own war between remaining at their soldier's side or retreating. Usually, even the strongest girls lasted only a few days and never more than a week. Eventually, the violent outbursts would break them. They would flee down the corridor in tears and simply not come back. He never spoke of those times to Noreen then, and trying to explain it now would appear self-serving. It was simply easier to let his wife believe he never liked Casey, rather than trying to explain he wanted to spare Carly the pain of having to run down that corridor in tears.

Turning into his driveway, Harlan saw the black Mustang convertible that had been Casey's pride and joy, the same car that Joe had only weeks ago deeded over to Carly, despite Harlan's objections. He parked the Chevy beside the car and started for the house.

Approaching the door, Harlan could hear his wife hysterically laughing while recounting her most recent trip to the senior center, where Mrs. McDonald had presented her with a sterling silver leaf pendant purchased on a recent trip to the casinos in Shreveport. Inside, Harlan found Noreen telling the story and peeling a bowl of new potatoes. Carly, attentive and chuckling along, was popping a bowl of snap beans.

"She didn't have a clue it was marijuana," Noreen said. "Had one just like it around her own neck in gold."

"Did you tell her?" Carly asked as Harlan entered the room.

"No, but she tried," he said. "Just wait. It gets better."

He kissed Carly on the cheek as Noreen tried to compose herself enough to finish the story. Harlan and Carly both watched patiently as Noreen blotted her eyes with the corner of a dishcloth, straining not to laugh.

"Well," Noreen began. She paused, inhaled deeply, and promptly lost what little composure she had mustered since Harlan returned. "She said, 'Marijuana? What's that?' So I said, 'It's like Mexican tobacco.' So she goes, 'Well, I never.' We all thought she was as shocked and surprised as we were and just dropped it. After all, she's a good Baptist and all. But that's not where the story ends. Harlan, you finish it."

"You think she'd at least have heard of pot," Harlan said with a chuckle. "Especially with that son of hers. But, no. I'm sitting at the house an hour later and get a phone call from the Sheriff. Seems Mrs. McDonald went wandering into the druggist for a pack of cigarettes. Asked for those 'Mary ones.' "

Carly gasped. "Uncle Harlan, she didn't!"

"Oh but she did. And you know how stubborn she is," he said. "So when the druggist insisted she must be mistaken, she–"

Noreen interrupted. "She proceeds to tell him that she knows what she's talking about because she's been smoking every day of her life and she wants to try marijuana now!"

"So Sheriff was there and very quietly explained to Mrs. McDonald what marijuana was," Noreen said, her voice finally calming a bit. "She took the necklace off right then and there and handed it to him. Said she didn't care what he did with it."

Carly laughed, her hand covering her mouth. "Poor Mrs. McDonald!"

Harlan poured himself a cup of coffee and sat down on the stool beside Carly and reached for a handful of beans. "So what's this news?"

Carly dropped her handful of beans back into the bowl, dusted her hands and folded them in her lap. When she didn't immediately answer Harlan tapped her shoulder. "You okay, sweetheart? It isn't bad, is it?"

"No, Uncle Harlan. Just, I don't want you to be disappointed," she said.

Noreen had stopped peeling potatoes and was staring across the counter. "Baby girl, you know you could never disappoint us."

"So, spill it, butter bean," Harlan said.

Carly smiled. "Well, I think I want to go to college."

Noreen shrieked. "That's wonderful!"

Harlan patted her knee. "So that's what all these trips were about? Austin and Dallas and San Antonio? Good girl. Decide to do something with your life."

She nodded, but then shook her head. "Yes, sir. But that's not it."

She produced a sketchbook from the bag beneath her stool. There was a bow tied around it. "This is your birthday gift. I did them all for you in the past few weeks."

Harlan removed the bow and began to flip through the pages of scenes from around Cranston. There was one of the sidewalk in front of Town Hall, of the Truck Stop Café, even three or four of the water tower over downtown. When he came to the last page, Harlan froze. It was a sketch of him, reading the paper at the Truck Stop Café.

He handed the book to Noreen, who thumbed the pages. "These are really good, baby," she said.

Harlan nodded his agreement. "I don't know what to say. When did you start drawing?"

"A long time ago. But I never thought I was any good. Casey always said–"

Noreen looked up with a start. "Casey knew?"

"He was the only one," Carly said. "So anyway. I've done hundreds of sketches like these. Maybe even thousands. And I've decided I'm going to art school."

Chapter Twelve

Doris watched the young banker sift through the brown expandable file in which she kept her entire financial history. Periodically, he would stop, his head cocked to the side, and slide a piece of paper half-way from its slot. Each time, after a cursory examination of whatever document grabbed his attention, he would drop it back into the folder. Not once had he removed any one of her financials all the way from the folder, and this gave Doris the distinct impression he was examining the folder only as a courtesy. Instead, as he leafed through her records, Doris became increasingly convinced the banker's computer had reduced her entire life to the single page lying face down and undisturbed atop the gleaming black printer on the credenza.

It was a scene she had already lived out during a similar meeting two days before at Cranston Bank and Trust, a visit that resulted in tears. Today's trip to Waco confirmed what she already knew. She didn't have the income to borrow the fifty thousand dollars to repair her house.

The banker closed the folder and removed his glasses, careful to avoid eye contact.

"So, Miss Greely. You get to Waco often?"

She sighed and reached for her purse.

"It's okay," she said as she gathered the folder and her purse. She stood to leave but the young banker stopped her.

"Miss Greely, I'm–"

"You're my second stop, son. I don't know why I came, really, since my own banker said no."

He forced a sympathetic smile. "I understand. You could try–"

"And waste their time too?"

His shoulders slumped and, with that, Doris knew he felt as defeated as she did. She turned to leave, but when she got to the door, he spoke.

"Miss Greely, it's this economy," he said flatly. "There just isn't any money to lend. And, honestly, I don't know we could give you a loan if we had it. You have good credit, but you simply don't have the income to carry a loan of that size."

In this Doris knew he was correct. Though she kept up with her bills, the weeks when she had much more than a few dollars left over were far apart. Even still, those weeks were more often than not punctuated by weeks in which Doris had to dip into her bank account to make up a shortfall. There was the family oil lease, which in its heyday had produced a comfortable living, but since had dwindled and now she was lucky if the royalty checks covered the water bill when they came in once a quarter. Where she would come up with the money to pay a house note, Doris hadn't considered. She wanted to confront the banker, to point out she had never been late on a bill and always paid off her debts. But she didn't. She excused herself without a word and returned to her car, unprepared for the trip back to Cranston, back to the café, to work Carly's afternoon shift.

She arrived at her car, tossed the folder and her purse absently into the back seat and climbed behind the wheel. The seat was hot against her back. Almost immediately she began to sweat. The air conditioner didn't help much and Doris realized she wasn't sweating due to the heat. She was shaking, angry, afraid to admit that the impulse coursing through her, the emotion taking hold at the base of her brain, was responsible for the white knuckles gripping the steering wheel: she could always run away.

People did it all the time. She grew up hearing stories about Bunny Carmichael, her mother's best friend. Bunny made a break for it when she was nineteen and never returned. She would phone Mama from time to time. But as the years wore on and Bunny's adventures took her ever farther away from Cranston, the calls grew less frequent until they eventually ceased. Nevertheless, her mother always called Bunny her best friend. Even though they never saw each other again, Doris knew her mother missed Bunny. Aside from Jimmy and Carly, though, who would miss her? Harlan would find someone else to bring him coffee. She could do it, she told herself. The only thing awaiting her in Cranston was a long evening shift after a long morning.

Just do it, just drive away and never look back.

Carly had been nice enough to take a morning shift after closing the night before. The last thing Doris should do was fail to uphold her end of the deal. Her hands began to relax against the wheel. A few seconds later, she put the car in drive and started the trip back home.

It was nearing two by the time Doris made the bend in Highway 7. From this direction, a stand of trees blocked the view of the abandoned truck stop, leaving a clear view of the glass and steel building. Despite clean lines gleaming in the sun, the café looked desolate. Someone had dropped it in the middle of a field and forgotten it there.

Doris steered her car into the mostly empty lot, parking beside Carly's Mustang. She pulled her red hair back into a tight bun and glanced in the mirror. She really should touch up her lipstick, but what would it matter? The evening shift rarely saw more than a couple of stray truckers and maybe one of the roughneck crews if Cranston was lucky enough to have a well going. She was about to step out of the car when she spied Carly through the window.

She was sitting in Joe's normal spot, hunched over a book, her finger tracing words as Téo Barros's lips moved. Absent Téo's dark complexion and black hair, it would have been easy to assume they were siblings. As Doris watched, Carly noticed her car and looked up and smiled and nudged Téo, who stopped reading. He waved at Doris, enthusiastic and beaming, to motion her inside. She suddenly felt ridiculous and needed an excuse for sitting in her car spying on them. She held up a finger and mouthed "just a second," before reaching in her purse for lipstick, then checked her face and started in.

A blast of cold air tinged with the pleasant, greasy aroma of hamburgers greeted her at the door. Téo stood and smiled and, for a moment, Doris almost thought he bowed. It was the same too-formal bearing of his father, and she was struck for the first time how similar the two appeared.

"Good afternoon, Téo. Whatcha working on today?"

"We are studying The Old Man and the Sea by Ernest Hemingway," he said. "Miss Carly says I should read aloud to improve my speaking."

"Sounds like it's working just fine. You keep at it."

He blushed and slid back in beside Carly.

"Mind if we stay and keep you company?" Carly asked. "Joe asked me to help out tutoring Téo."

Doris shook her head.

"I'll just be doing whatever it is you do on the night shift. You ain't in my way," she said. The truth was, she was quite happy for them to stay. She knew the book, read it in high school and enjoyed it. Listening to Téo read would be a more-than-welcome distraction from the disappointments of the day. Maybe if she could clear her mind, a plan might present itself and all would be well. So Doris replenished the napkin dispensers and refilled salt and pepper shakers to the tale of Santiago and the great fish. Listening to the boy read the words through a thick accent made the story that much more real. Somewhere around mid-afternoon, as the sun settled into the deep red of the pasture across the highway, Téo became Manolin narrating the Old Man's trial and Doris found her mind straying away from the café to the skiff on the Gulf Stream.

With Santiago's return to the dock, Jimmy popped his head in from the kitchen. "What you say we shut her down early, call it a day?"

Doris shrugged.

Ten minutes later, she was in her driveway, staring up at her house. Night had fallen and it was difficult to make out the four columns towering twenty feet up over the porch. None of the windows were illuminated and there was no moon to shine down. Were it not for the single bare bulb glaring by the front door, the house would have been little more than a dark hole in the blackness of the night.

Chapter Thirteen

A week after his first visit, Harlan arrived at the back corner of his property early enough to watch the first hints of sun reach over the distant tree line of the Bartley homeplace and spread its rays over the pasture between his property and Ted and Margie's house a half-mile away. The original breach spanned only a few feet, but he had discovered the wood rotten for ten yards and came prepared for an extra ten feet beyond that. Just the demolition alone would take at least an hour longer than it would have taken with his father's hammer, no thanks to the new composite hammer, Harlan convinced himself. Nevertheless, Harlan pressed on, pulling nails and piling lumber. When at last he was ready to begin hanging the new fence rails, he heard an ATV motor approaching in the distance and looked up.

Ted brought the four-wheeler to a stop on his side of the fence and hopped off, dusting his pants. "You're up early."

"Been up since five, same as usual," Harlan said. He struggled for a moment to get the new rail propped against the post. Ted moved in to assist, but Harlan shook his head. "Grab the other end, help keep it level."

Ted complied without protest, leveled the rail and held it in place as Harlan set the first nails. As Harlan finished up mounting the first rail, Ted eyed the stack of two-bys in the back of Harlan's Chevy.

"Boy, that must have set you back a penny," Ted said.

"About three hundred dollars' worth," Harlan said.

Ted set out a long whistle. "That's a lot of money to fix a fence."

"Things cost what they cost."

"You could have just left it open, you know?"

Harlan stopped driving the latest nail and looked up at Ted, perplexed. "And what? Leave a broken fence?"

"Why we need a fence? I ain't got cows. Neither have you, last I checked."

Harlan shrugged. "Fence is busted, you gotta fix it. It's just what you do. Good fences, you know?"

Harlan was glad when Ted accepted the explanation without further protest. If he was comfortable spending his money to fix an unnecessary fence, what business was it of Ted's? Besides, three hundred dollars for more lumber and nails was the least issue on his mind. He still had not come to grips with his niece's desire to go to college. That was the reason he had been so eager to get back to the pasture, and having found none of the resolution he sought, with the late-spring sun beating down upon him, Harlan was pleased Ted had decided to turn up.

"Art school," Harlan mumbled under his breath. "Sorry I'm short with you this morning, Ted. But it's art school."

"Carly?"

Harlan looked up, surprised. "You knew?"

"Margie overheard her talking to Doris about it the other day, at the café. Said she was looking at UT?"

Harlan nodded, silent as Ted continued, "I don't get it. I mean, I could understand teaching or nursing. They're respectable, solid career choices for a young woman in Carly's situation. What the hell's she going to do with an art degree, Harlan?"

Harlan shrugged. It was the question he'd been asking himself all morning. "Be an artist, she says. Waste of damned money, you ask me."

"And that's another thing. How's she going to pay for it?"

"She doesn't know yet," he replied, his tone mocking Carly's insistence it wouldn't cost her mother to send her. "She says she'll do scholarships and loans to pay for it, continue working. I tried to tell her."

"Kids these days," Ted said, shaking his head.

"Kids my ass. She's twenty, for Pete's sake. Twenty and decides now she's going to college?" Harlan tossed the hammer to the ground in disgust and leaned across the newly installed rail. "When I was her age, I was in the Army and had already put in another five working for Daddy. Hell. Noreen and I had been married a year."

"Tell me about it," Ted replied. "Think this has anything to do with the Morton boy?"

Harlan snorted. "Doesn't everything these days?"

"You heard the latest?"

Harlan dusted the hammer off as he reached for another nail. "What now?"

"Truck arrived from Amarillo yesterday, loaded down with angle-iron," Ted said. "Well, aluminum, I'd imagine. But yeah. Unloaded the whole flatbed into Creedmore's place. Made that Mexican and his son tote the whole mess of it inside."

Harlan drove another nail. "How much angle-iron?"

"A lot. We watched them work for the better part of the morning just to unload it."

Harlan dug a squashed Red Man pouch from his back pocket and pinched off a neat plug. He tucked the wad of tobacco in his cheek, taking in this latest news.

"What do you think Joe's up to with those kind of materials?" Ted asked finally.

Harlan spat into the dirt. "No good."

Chapter Fourteen

Harlan slammed the small brass door shut and tucked the stack of envelopes under his arm before locking the box with a sigh. A trip to the post office normally relaxed Harlan. He took comfort in the cold austerity of the too-high ceilings. The marble and granite lent strength and permanence and steadiness. This particular morning, even after four trips to the fence, he found himself still completely without answers to his questions about Joe and that Mexican and his niece's bent for art school. All three were connected and he was going to figure out how. Walking into the Truck Stop Café, he was itching to hold a sit-down with Joe. He settled into his normal seat in the corner, turned the empty cup mouth up in the saucer, and waited.

Each time the bells clattered against the door, he would look up from the Sun-Times only to be disappointed yet again. The morning crew came and went without so much as a word about Creedmore's and Joe, their banter instead restrained to talk of the upcoming Summer Carnival and Bazaar. He finished the paper and started in on the stack of mail, though he did not expect to make much sense out of the half-dozen "explanation of benefits" forms or the bills from the V.A. He gave up and reached for a discarded Dallas newspaper someone had left on the table beside him. On page three, Harlan found an A.P. report on the latest terror attacks in Baghdad. Harlan shook his head with a tisk.

"Three more boys yesterday," he said. "And it didn't even make the front page. God bless America."

The silence with which this interjection was greeted surprised him and he looked up from the paper to find the pipeline boys sitting at the bar focused on the sports ticker scrolling by at the bottom of the muted television above the counter. Harlan noisily rattled the paper to display his disapproval. When even that terseness drew no response, he shook his head and resigned himself to the morning.

"More coffee, Harlan?" Doris asked him after he had folded the paper and tossed it into the empty bench across from him.

He nodded.

"Anything else?" she asked before leaving.

He waved her off, but then stopped her. "What time you seeing Joe these days?"

"Ain't."

"He don't come no more?"

"No. He's not been coming to breakfast. Comes to dinner about two thirty, instead," she said.

"He's coming here? For lunch?"

Doris grumbled something under her breath and wandered away from the table. Harlan called after her, "Here? For lunch? Why so late?"

Doris craned her neck around the corner from the kitchen. "Harlan, if you are so damned concerned about it, stick around and ask him yourself."

The doorbells clattered to life and Harlan looked up to find the Mexican and his boy in the doorway. Doris reemerged from the kitchen and smiled. "Welcome back, Mr. Barros, Téo."

Harlan's ears perked. Back? How often had they been coming in? And why the hell was Doris so chipper about their visit?

"Thank you, Miss Doris. We will not be too much trouble. Téo has homework he must complete before we work today."

Harlan cleared his throat. "And what sort of work do you do?"

The man smiled when he talked. "I work for Mr. Joe at the furniture store."

"Planning on selling a lot of furniture, are you?"

Something about the way the Mexican smiled back when he answered disconcerted Harlan. Even though the man had not answered his question, Harlan did not press the issue. Instead, he just nodded once. The man ushered his son into a booth near the door before approaching Harlan's corner perch, hand extended.

"I am sorry if I have offended you in some way."

Harlan took the man's hand so firmly he felt knuckles grinding together beneath the leathery flesh. "Nope. Just not much for outsiders is all."

"You remember of course my son, Téo. I come to help him study, Mr. Cotton."

"Call me Harlan."

"Thank you, Harlan." Vítor said. "This is a lovely town in which to live. I think maybe this town is heaven?"

When Vítor smiled a second time, Harlan was again taken aback. It was as if the smile conveyed the purity of the emotion behind it. There was no malice, no sarcasm, no hidden wit. It was the smile of a man who, in that moment, was utterly happy and, in Harlan's world, no one experienced such emotions so purely. Or if they did, they kept it to themselves. But since Vítor Barros had expressed his approval of Cranston, Harlan could not outright dismiss the man before him as unintelligent. He decided to probe deeper, but their moment was interrupted when Téo called out to his father in a foreign language.

"Pai, eu ñao comprendo."

Vítor turned to his son, speaking to the boy in a hushed tone. "English, Téo, please. It is rude to speak such before those who do not understand you. This is our country now and here, we must speak this language."

"But Pai, I do not understand the questions in this book," the boy said, his voice thick with the accent of his father.

Vítor bowed to Harlan and again extended his hand. "Forgive me the rudeness, Harlan. My son. He is how do you say... schooled at home? I teach him my trade as well as mathematics, reading, and science. We shall talk again, yes?"

Harlan shook Vítor's hand with a nod. Yes, he told himself, we will definitely speak again. He watched as the man folded his tall frame into the small booth beside Téo and hunkered down over the textbook. Doris arrived to refill Harlan's coffee, but he placed his hand atop the cup.

"That'll be all, darlin'," he said. "Places to go, people to see."

As she returned to her customary spot behind the counter, near the pie case, Harlan pulled himself out of the corner booth and started for the door. He stopped at the counter and motioned her closer to him.

"Doris, put Barros's bill on my tab, please."

She shot him a wary eye. "That's mighty nice of you."

He winked. "Just trying to do the neighborly thing, Doris."

Tipping his hat to Vítor Barros and Téo, Harlan left the diner with a new angle on the Joe Morton issue. Once behind the wheel, Harlan pointed the Chevy down the highway towards town and fumbled for his cell phone. He dialed a number from memory and waited for the answer. After several rings, voicemail.

"This is John Shepard. If this is a personal call, leave a message. If it's town business, call city hall," the mayor's voice told him. Harlan tossed the phone on the seat without leaving a message. The mayor would know what he was calling about.

Chapter Fifteen

The next morning, two things happened that took his mind off Joe Morton and the Mexican for a while. First, while Harlan was out for a morning horseback ride, Viking's bridle snapped and Harlan thought he was going to be thrown. It took more than a little skill and effort, but he quickly settled himself back into the saddle and was able to dismount without injury. The second distraction that morning came with the morning mail and it was addressed not to Harlan or Noreen Cotton, but to Ms. Carly Machen.

This was the fourth or fifth such envelope to arrive in a week, and for the first time, Harlan began to realize that Carly meant to follow through with her plans to attend art school.

"Where is Vanderbilt, anyway?" Noreen asked, running her fingers over the return address.

"Tennessee," he replied flatly before kissing her cheek and heading for the door.

"Well, at least it's closer than New York," she had said with a sigh.

Driving out to the feed store an hour later, Harlan still couldn't find much of a difference. Tennessee, New York, Los Angeles. While they were all very different cities, they were all the same. They weren't Cranston. He turned on the radio and tuned it to a talk radio station just in time to hear the last few seconds of a report on corn futures before the regular program returned.

"Before the break, I told you we'd be talking with retired Army Brigadier General David Nordickar about the latest successes of our boys in Iraq," the host said. "General, welcome to the show. The air is yours."

"Thank you," Nordickar said. "And thank you to your listeners for all of the kind things they are saying about my book."

"It's a great book from a great American," the host said.

"Well, thank you again. But today, I just got off the phone with a couple of my colleagues over there. And while I can't tell you too much, I have to brag about the success we're seeing," the General said. "I believe we're on the verge of an unconditional victory."

The host interrupted. "I know what that means to me and what it means to you, General. But tell our listeners, if you would. What is an unconditional victory in Iraq?"

Harlan and the General answered simultaneously, "Democracy."

Harlan self-assuredly smacked the steering wheel. "Damned straight."

The general began rattling off troop numbers and Arabic neighborhoods in Baghdad so quickly that Harlan couldn't keep up and, for the briefest of moments, Harlan lost concentration, his eyes settling on the parking lot of the Truck Stop Café and a black Mustang in the parking lot. Almost instinctively, Harlan wheeled into the café and brought the Chevy to a stop in between the Mustang and Joe's pickup.

Through the windows, he spied the pair sitting in Joe's customary booth, Joe absently thumbing through one of Carly's ubiquitous sketchbooks as she animatedly chattered away. Harlan couldn't help but notice the ease with which she and Joe interacted. It was the first time since Casey's death he had seen her genuinely relaxed. Likewise, Joe was reclined in the booth, his back resting against the glass, his legs stretched out on the bench before him. The absurdity of this paranoid spying hit Harlan suddenly and he froze, his hand resting on the gear shift. Before he could flee, Carly's eyes met his and she smiled at him. With his only avenue for anonymous escape gone, he killed the engine and headed in.

"Afternoon, Uncle Harlan," she said as he approached the booth.

She scooted towards the window to make room for him in the booth. He slid in beside her, kissing her on the cheek. "Afternoon, Joe. Didn't mean to interrupt your meeting."

"Not at all," Joe said. "Carly was just showing me some of her drawings."

"What gets into kids, these days?" Harlan said without thinking. He immediately winced but relaxed a little when he saw Joe had not reacted. He quickly tried to change the subject. "So what brings you two together today?"

"Well," Carly began. "Mr. Joe offered me a job."

"A job? What kind of job?"

Joe cleared his throat. "Relax, Harlan. Téo Barros needs an English tutor. Thought I'd pay Carly here a little extra money to do it."

"What, he can't just go to school like the rest of the kids?"

"Uncle Harlan, you've met him. He's not from here. He doesn't speak the language very well."

Harlan sat silently for a moment. He didn't have anything against the Mexican's boy. Téo couldn't help where he was born any more than he could control where his father dragged him. But Carly was an altogether different story. She had been his responsibility since her father had walked out and now, yet again, he was finding out just how distant she had grown in the months since Casey's death. Less than a week ago she was talking about college in the fall. Now she was taking on students? Truth be known, he thought, he couldn't decide which was worse–wanting to go to away to college or wanting to teach a wetback to talk American.

"What about school?" he asked aloud.

She laughed. "It's only for a few months, silly. They aren't going to live here forever."

For the briefest of moments, Harlan wished they were permanent additions. At least that way, Carly stood the chance of getting attached to the boy and deciding to remain behind as his tutor until, at last, she would be too old to go running off to some art school. Then, she'd remain in Cranston. He flinched when he felt Carly rest a cool, reassuring hand on his forearm.

"Uncle Harlan, are you okay?"

He nodded unconvincingly.

"Don't worry, Harlan," Joe said. "It's not like tutoring the Barros boy will take her away from you."

Chapter Sixteen

When he was sixteen, Harlan's father gave him two gifts on the same day: a summer job stomping trailers at a Louisiana cotton farm run by a family friend and a mechanical alarm clock that required winding each night before bed. He remembered fondly the mornings spent in the cabin by the pond. Rising early, the farmer's wife served a stout breakfast and stouter coffee. After a day in the fields, Harlan would return to the cabin, where he would bathe, eat the dinner the farmer's wife had left him, and wind the clock before turning in for the night.

In the years since, Harlan's routine at bed had never varied. He would wind the clock, set the alarm for six, kiss Noreen before rolling over, and sleep until rising the next morning, making sure to be awake before the alarm could rouse him. Not once in more than thirty years of marriage had Noreen ever heard the bell ring.

As the weeks of spring unfolded and Harlan entered his summer routine, he began to relish the mornings in the barn beside the house, time spent with his three horses. At first, Harlan wasn't aware of the extra time he was spending in the barn. He felt more rushed in the trips into town for breakfast each day. Not until one morning, when his cell phone rang and Ted asked why he wasn't at the Café yet did Harlan realize it was after ten and he'd been with the horses for three hours. The morning following, he awoke with the intention of taking less than half an hour to let the horses out of their stalls and into the corral for the morning. But by eight thirty, he no longer cared whether or not he made it to breakfast before the crowd left. Over a cup of coffee that evening, he had broached the subject with Noreen.

"Maybe you need some time away from the Café?" she offered.

"Maybe so," he had replied.

Harlan was thankful Noreen didn't bother to point out the horses might represent the times he had spent with Carly, though he knew his wife recognized that's what it was. The horses had always been theirs, ever since Carly's mother had moved to Florida, leaving behind a daughter who refused to leave her friends. Even before that, if he thought about it. Mornings in the barn had calmed him down, quelled racing thoughts and occupied his mind with something other than whatever was bothering him. Of late, though, the horses had become a nagging reminder of all three of his problems and one of them more than the others. After all, where was Carly now?

One Tuesday morning in mid-June, Harlan was in the truck, heading to breakfast after a particularly invigorating morning with the horses. Turning onto Main Street, he came to a stop in the middle of the road, just up from the Creedmore Building.

Had it been there before?

No, he shook his head. He was sure it was a new addition. There had never been a flagpole atop the building. But here it was, writ larger than life. Harlan could tell from the colors, the stiff way in which the fabric coiled and uncoiled, folded in on itself and then released, this was not a cheap flag. In fact, Harlan wouldn't have to ask where Joe had gotten this particular flag.

His cell phone rang for the fourth time this morning, and as he had done with three previous interruptions, he silenced it without looking to see who was calling him. He tossed the phone back onto the dashboard and leaned up on the steering wheel, peering up at Casey's flag.

His phone rang again and, before he silenced it, Harlan saw it was the mayor calling. He flipped the phone open and grunted.

"Hello?"

"Harlan, Shep here," the mayor said. "You coming to breakfast?"

"I'm on my way there now, but I'm looking at–" he began. The mayor cut him off.

"Good. Get here right quick, brother. We've got a problem."

"What sort of problem, Shep?"

"Just get here quick. It's about the Independence Day festival."

Harlan opened his mouth to reply, but the mayor had already hung up. Through the windshield, Harlan eyed Casey's flag and grunted again. What kind of father would fly that flag?

And there, at the corner of Norris and Main, Harlan finally connected everything. Carly's stack of acceptance letters to art school, Joe's plans for the Creedmore Building, and that Mexican, Vítor Barros, weren't separate issues. They were all part of the same, complex equation. As Harlan dropped the Chevy back into drive and squealed the tires without checking his mirrors, he eyed the top of the building one last time, where the single biggest clue to the strange affair of Joe Morton wafted defiantly in the breeze.

Chapter Seventeen

"No one expected gas prices to do this, Harlan. You don't know what it's been like, brother."

Since Harlan had arrived twenty minutes before, Shep had been forced to repeat all the details of the morning's discussions again. Rising gas prices had forced budget overruns in the fire department and the police department. More than five thousand and change, Shep told him. And that meant there just wasn't money for the annual fireworks display.

"Ain't no one's fault, Harlan," Ted offered.

Harlan ignored him. "But it's tradition. We'll just have to find the money."

"These are tight times, Harlan," said Frederick Gruber. "Even in my business we're cutting back."

"Fireworks are a luxury we just can't afford this year, Harlan," Shep said. "It isn't so much open for discussion as it was just a for-your-information."

Shep wished he hadn't expected Harlan's reaction. But so far, his old friend's performance was right on cue. Truth told, Shep had been glad to find Harlan wasn't there when he arrived that morning to spread the word. It had given the mayor sufficient time to explain the precarious financial state of several Cranston departments before the ensuing controversy. The look on Harlan's face told Shep that he had misjudged the power of his reinforcements.

"How much are we short, mayor? Maybe we could raise the money private-like," Harlan said.

The mayor shook his head. "Fireworks guys said it will cost us fifteen grand–five more than last year, and we'd have to guarantee them the spot to get them to book. I don't much see we can get the money together in two weeks."

"Rotary?" Harlan asked.

Ted shook his head. "No can do, brother. Casey's service tapped us out."

Harlan folded his arms in a huff. "It just ain't right."

"No one is saying it is, Harlan. But face it. What would you rather have, fireworks or fire trucks?" Shep smiled, pleased at the impromptu wit he'd just pulled off. He hoped it would be enough to put the fireworks discussion to bed once and for all.

For two months, he had wondered how this morning would go for him, how he'd tell Harlan. He really did understand why his friend felt so strongly. After all, traditions in Cranston ran long and strong. Let something upset the tradition and it became a recipe for all kinds of controversy–controversy Shep would just as soon avoid this late in his career. He hadn't told anyone yet, but this would be his last term as mayor. For years now, his wife had been goading him to retire from public life so they could travel. "We'll buy one of them RVs and go see the grandkids," she frequently said. She had even picked out the model she wanted, proclaiming frequently, "It has real granite counters!"

At that moment, in the Truck Stop Café, Shep wished he had listened to her three years ago before saying to himself, "one last term." Alas, he hadn't and now, here he sat, a confounded failure. The annual Cranston Fireworks on the Fourth would die with his tenure. It was a failure he wished he did not have to bear.

Shep's gaze returned to Harlan. He watched the man sitting in the corner, where he could be found every morning, and tried to discern what he was thinking. "Harlan, buddy. We'll bring them back next year," Shep said, but he quickly realized Harlan wasn't paying attention.

He glanced over his shoulder to see what it was that held Harlan so transfixed and there, sitting at the opposite end of the Café, Vítor Barros was hunched over a book with his son. The boy was chattering nervously with Barros in a language Shep didn't recognize.

"Que é dia de independência, papai?" the boy asked for a second time.

"É o aniversário do país," his father replied.

Harlan stood up, his face red with anger. "I can't think with all that damned clackity-clack chatter down there."

All the men gathered around Harlan's corner booth tensed. Shep moved to stop Harlan from stepping out, but he was interrupted by Barros himself.

"Forgive my son, Mr. Cotton. His English is not very good."

"What the hell is he on about down there, anyway?" Harlan demanded.

At any moment, Shep expected, Barros would charge and tackle Harlan. There would be a fight. The law would be called and reports would have to be filed. "Harlan's done gone and done it now," he could hear Doris saying the next morning. But the man didn't charge.

Instead, he approached quietly and smiled. "He did not know about the Independence Day, what it represents. I was attempting to explain it to him."

He gestured for Téo to join him. When the boy arrived at his side, he placed his arm around his shoulders. "Téo, you remember Mr. Cotton, yes?"

"Sim, pai."

Barros jarred the boy. "English, Téo. This is our country now. You must learn English."

"Yes, papa. I remember him."

Harlan had not stepped away from the booth, but he hadn't settled back into his seat either. Shep was still there, ready to spring into the void between the two men, should a fight break out. However, Barros was proving quite the diplomat.

"I was explaining to Téo about the Independence Day, what it means in America. He is disappointed for the fireworks," Barros told Harlan.

Harlan snorted. "Damned Mexicans. Come up here thinking it's y'all's country."

Barros smiled again. This time, Harlan took a step forward.

"What you smiling at, son?"

"Forgive me, Mr. Cotton. But we are not Mexicans. We are from Brazil."

"But you was speaking Mexican, weren't you?"

"No, sir. We were speaking Portuguese. It is our native language," Barros replied.

Shep raised his hand to Harlan. "See, brother. He wasn't talking bad about Noreen after all."

The men all laughed nervously, but the moment of humor brought enough levity that Harlan finally sat back down.

"Tell the boy I'm sorry about the fireworks," Harlan said, as if Téo would not have understood.

Barros motioned for Téo to return to their table. "Go study, son. I will be right there."

When his son was safely out of earshot, Vítor turned back to the men. "I am sorry. He misses home. Sometimes, he speaks in his old language. It is a most rude habit I am working diligently to correct."

"It's not a big deal," Shep said. He quickly shot a look across the table to silence Harlan. "After all, this is your country, too, I guess."

"Yes. We are both citizens, Téo and I. Téo for just a few months but me, for more than twenty-five years."

Ted's ears perked. "That long? What brought you over here?"

"Work, mostly. During Vietnam, I joined the United States Navy to go to college. That helped me achieve citizenship," Vítor said. He pointed to Téo. "He took me back to Brazil for a while, where I worked to take care of his mother. But I missed America, so I came back to work here again. When she died last year, Téo came to live with me."

Shep kicked Harlan under the table. "See there. Navy man. You should be ashamed of yourself."

Harlan didn't respond. Instead, he continued to stare off into space, lost in some thought or another. Shep shrugged it off.

"Well, Mr. Barros. I am very sorry Téo's first Fourth of July in America will be without fireworks. Maybe next year."

Vítor's lips turned up into something resembling a smile. "Perhaps, yes. Good day, gentlemen."

Shep watched the tall Brazilian navigate his way across the Café and sit back down. The mayor checked his watch and shook his head.

"Sorry boys. Gotta get to the office."

"Mayor," Harlan said, stopping him. "Would you mind if I took a look at the books? Maybe I can find the money somewhere else?"

Shep had expected this request and had come prepared. He reached into his briefcase and removed a folder, thick with bound pages. "Here. Use my copy of the city budget. Let me know if you find anything."

Harlan took the folder, nodding. "I will. You say we have to let the fireworks company know by tomorrow?"

"That's right."

"Well, I'll get right on this, then," Harlan said.

Chapter Eighteen

The mayor's copy of the budget, the pages now dog-eared and the margins filled with pencil scratches, lay open on the table before Harlan. Doris wandered by with a carafe and filled the cup he had just emptied. He had been alone all morning and, as if they knew better than to take their customary seats in the corner booth, the breakfast crowd had avoided sitting with him as he examined columns of numbers and filled page after page of a yellow legal pad with notes about squeezing the overtime budget of the public works department to save another fifty.

Harlan had spent at least ten hours studying the budget and had managed to scrounge together only eight hundred dollars. For all his faults, the mayor wasn't wrong. It was a very tight budget and Harlan made a mental note to commend Shep on his fiscal skill.

Harlan was lost in the town's waterworks budget when he noticed he was no longer alone. He looked up and almost did a double take when he saw the face of Vítor Barros smiling back.

"Good morning, Mr. Cotton," Vítor said.

Harlan grunted his reply, hoping his gruffness was enough of a clue that he wished to be left alone. When Vítor did not immediately move to leave, Harlan peered at him over the rim of his readers. "What can I do for you today?"

"It is a glorious morning, is it not?"

Harlan tossed his glasses onto the table. "What on earth are you talking about?"

Vítor gestured to the windows. "The sun is shining. There are birds singing. The day. It is beautiful, yes?"

"I'm very busy, Mr. Barros. If you would please excuse–"

"Yes, with the fireworks display. The whole of Cranston is speaking of the matter," Vítor said. He smiled that toothy, big smile that said to Harlan the man knew more than he was willing to let on.

Harlan picked up his glasses and put them back on, hunched close to the notebook and attempted to brush the interloper off. But Vítor did not seem to notice or decided against taking the hint.

"My Téo. He is very disappointed there will be no fireworks. He has been almost crying about it all day and all night. Even Mr. Joe, he voices his endless unhappiness about the matter."

Harlan heaved a sigh and looked up again. "Yes, I get it. Everyone is disappointed, Mr. Barros. But I'm trying to do something about that, if people would leave me be."

Vítor again nodded, his face stern and serious. Finally, he was beginning to comprehend that his presence was unwanted, Harlan thought. But the man still continued.

"Of course, Mr. Cotton. Have you made any progress?"

"Some, but not enough. I could be making a lot more, though, if you people'd just leave me be already," Harlan said, a bit too forcefully.

"Of course, Mr. Cotton," he said. He slid to the edge of his seat and wavered, as if he had momentarily forgotten whether or not he had left the oven on. He opened his mouth to speak, but decided against it and rose to leave. Before he took the first step, though, he stopped and rested his hand on the corner of the table.

"Mr. Cotton?" he said.

Harlan had to crane is neck to look up at the figure towering over him. Eyebrows raised, Harlan grunted. "Yes?"

Vítor reached into the pocket of his sports coat and removed an envelope. He held it between his fingers, studying it for a moment before offering it to Harlan.

"With the compliments of Mr. Joe," Vítor said as Harlan took the envelope from his hand.

He bowed slightly, smiled again, and tipped his hat at Doris as he left. Harlan watched as he pulled away from the parking lot and headed back to town. Harlan was absently fingering the corner of the envelope when Doris approached with a fresh pot of coffee.

"What was that about?" she asked, filling his cup.

"He handed me this," Harlan replied. She eyed the unopened envelope.

"What is it?"

He shrugged, silent.

"Well, open it!"

Harlan slid his finger along the flap, separating the seal. He removed a single sliver of green paper. Harlan nearly choked when he saw the face of the check.

"What the hell is it?" Doris asked.

When he didn't break his stunned silence, she reached for the check herself. It was drawn from Joe Morton's account at Cranston State Bank, and Doris swooned when she saw the amount. Joe's check was made out to the Town of Cranston in the amount of twenty thousand dollars. The memo line read, simply, "For Téo's fireworks."

Doris handed the check back to Harlan and rubbed her fingers, as if the check had left some magical residue on them. She and Harlan looked at one another for several seconds before she chuckled.

"Well I'll be goddamned," she said, walking away.

Chapter Nineteen

Word of Joe's generosity spread through Cranston like a brush-fire. Within hours, the entire population had converged on the diner, at the beauty shop or in front of the pharmacy counter, chattering away about the upcoming fireworks display, and it didn't take long for them to connect the Independence Day celebration with whatever Joe had going up on the roof of the Creedmore Building. For weeks, the whine of saws and clang of hammers had drawn their eyes to the rooftop, only to reward them with an empty sky. To the townsfolk, Joe's check was as much an announcement of his intent to unveil his secret project as it was a generous effort to ensure that Téo would get his fireworks on his first Independence Day.

No matter how they looked at it, though, Joe's sudden generosity created an instant air of mystery. A few days after Vítor Barros delivered the check to Harlan, Joey Caldwell and Carl Harding, two boys from the high school, hopped a security fence and climbed up the water tower, the only vantage point high enough to offer a clear line of sight to the rooftops. They had hoped to shed light on the mystery, but what they described when they came down only added questions. Spreading out across the roof was a web of interconnected angle-iron, wires and sheet metal. The boys had watched for more than an hour as Joe assisted Vítor and Téo welding the pieces together into a large grid.

"I'm telling you, no good will come of this," Ted warned the mayor. "None at all."

Shep ignored the warning. "Whatever Joe's up to, I'm sure it's nothing," he replied and returned to planning the celebrations.

The breakfast crowd took to treating Harlan as a returning hero. In the last week of June, the crowd was gathered around him at the corner table, speculating about Joe's plans for the Fourth. It was the morning Harlan's attention would be diverted once and for all from the metalwork atop Creedmore's, but as Margie quizzed him about the size of the display, he was still enjoying his time as man of the hour.

"Five extra thousand dollars? How many more minutes is that?" she asked.

Harlan smiled. "A full ten minutes. Also, they are bringing a big sound system and are going to play the 1812 Overture."

Even Frederick Gruber was having trouble masking his excitement. "I remember seeing the fireworks in Austin with the children. They play that music there, as well."

"Should we have more flags?" Greg Johnston asked. "I have some extra pipe."

Harlan shook him off. "No, the dozen is enough. No need to be ostentatious."

"What about a reading of the names?" someone near the back of the group suggested.

Harlan looked up and saw it was one of the Franklin brothers, though he had never been able to tell them apart.

"Names, Jerry?" he asked, taking a stab.

"Gary. Yeah, you know," Gary said. "Like they do with September eleventh? Read the names of the fallen soldiers?"

"Do any of you have a clue how many people that is?" came an incredulous voice from the counter. Doris had returned from the kitchen, her arms laden with fresh pies.

When they all returned a similar, blank stare, Doris shook her head. "More than three thousand names. You gonna read all those people off, Gary?"

He didn't answer.

"Anyone else?"

They remained silent for a moment and she continued to place the pies in the pie case. She stopped momentarily and shot Harlan a look.

"You're sitting up in here, the queen bee king of the hill, like you did something special and all you did was show up for breakfast."

"Doris, that ain't fair," Margie said. Doris ignored her.

"I'll bet not a one of you has bothered to call up Joe and thank him, have you? Or maybe gone by and took him a cup of coffee?" She looked from person to person, waiting for some hint of protest on their faces. When none came, she sighed. "I should have figured as much."

Doris placed the final pie under the dome on the counter, dusted her hands and stormed from the room. She paced the parking lot behind the Café, the merciless east Texas sun pressing down as she puffed away at a cigarette. She wanted to scream, to curse them all. First, Casey's funeral, now the fireworks. The whole year had left Doris wondering what these people had done with their brains. And who died and made Harlan Cotton king? Sitting there, holding court, running the town the way he liked. Even the way he was treating his niece had become a sore point to Doris. Here the girl wants to go to art school, do something meaningful with her life. But he pushes her down and browbeats her. Thinking about Carly made her smile, though. The girl would get her day and so would–much sooner than he was expecting. She recognized in Carly the emotion that would drive the girl to rebellion against her uncle, against everything that Cranston seemed to stand for, and Doris was thankful for Carly's willpower. At the same time, Doris was afraid because it meant she recognized in herself the emotion driving Carly away.

Confinement.

The easy, regimented life Doris had come to love, the picnics and the familiarity, the church life and the politics, all of it had compounded in recent years and transformed from a cloister into a prison. It was Carly Machen's strength to escape that same prison that Doris so loved. There was a name for such emotional connections, but Doris couldn't recall it. She would have given anything to be rid of the family house, the land, the history. To just throw it all up in the air.

Thoughts of the house made her chuckle. That was a problem that would take care of itself soon enough. She had moved her bed into the dining room, but if the contractor was right, the house would become completely uninhabitable within a year or two.

She stubbed her cigarette out on the heel of her shoe and flicked the butt into the ashtray beside the kitchen door. By the time she returned to the dining room, everyone had gone, save Harlan, who was sitting in the corner booth staring out across the parking lot. His cell phone was lying on the table, ringing.

Doris called across the bar, "Hey, answer that."

He shook his head. "Nah. It's just Noreen."

Doris knew why Noreen was calling. She knew Carly had shared with her aunt that morning what she'd told Doris last night. By the end of the summer, Carly was moving to Austin. Though completely expected, the news excited Doris almost to no end. Carly's life was set to unfold far away from the smallness that was Cranston, away from Harlan and Noreen.

Suddenly, Doris saw Harlan in a different light, a man intent on keeping his world just so, not out of some misguided desire for control but as a tool for self-defense. He had been good to Carly and always tried to keep her best interests in mind as he steered her through a fragile youth. First came the death of her father. Then, when her mother moved to Florida, it was Harlan who suggested Carly remain in Cranston to finish high school. Harlan encouraged caution in her relationship with Casey, not because he disliked the boy, but because he understood what war was about and wanted to spare his niece the pain of such a loss.

As Harlan's unanswered cell phone rang away on the table, its message undelivered, Doris began to regret the moment she just spent gloating about his pending loss. Her pride in Carly's tenacity undiminished, she nevertheless felt sorry for Harlan, whose life she now understood was driven not by a need to control but by the deep love of a man for his family, for his town. And in that moment, she finally understood the metamorphosis Harlan faced as he reached to answer Noreen's call.

Chapter Twenty

Harlan drummed his fingers impatiently on the steering wheel, reluctant to go into his own home for fear of another confrontation. In the days since Carly announced she would begin classes at UT in the fall, things had not been going so well around the Cotton household. Every meal became a battle fought over the dinner table and more than one meal had ended with Noreen fleeing the fighting in tears. Sitting in his driveway, Harlan did not expect this lunch visit to be much different.

He killed the ignition with a sigh and started for the house. The kitchen door was ajar, and he could hear the sound of water running into the sink and smell the turnip greens on the stove. He paused, staring in through the screen door and watched his niece move silently about the kitchen, passing to his wife first a loaf of bread from the cupboard and then a jar of mayonnaise from the fridge. Neither spoke to the other, and Harlan was sure that he could feel the tension between them.

Noreen saw him through the screen and forced a smile. "You almost missed lunch."

"Sorry," he replied, though he wasn't sure why he felt the need to apologize. He wasn't late. In fact, he was a full twenty minutes earlier than he had expected to be. Yet here he was, standing at the door, as if he needed to knock to enter his own home.

"You gonna come in or not?" Noreen said.

"Oh, yeah," he said. He tried the latch but it was locked.

Carly rushed over, opened the screen and stepped well out of his way to allow him entry.

"Sorry. I latched it because the dogs kept trying to go out," she said.

He leaned in and kissed her cheek. "So what's for lunch?"

"Sandwiches," Noreen said. "I got some of that really good ham from Robertson's and Margie brought us over some fresh tomatoes from her garden."

"That'll be nice," Harlan said. He took his seat at the table and opened up the Sun-Times. Reading the paper a second time would be far less trouble than trying to avoid conversation. No matter what they decided to discuss, he knew art school would be the subtext and that, inevitably, they would come to words and, after a week of listening to it, he didn't have any energy left.

Noreen set a plate on the table before him. Harlan folded the paper and rested it beside his plate. Carly took the chair next to him just as Noreen sat down at her own place. The trio ate in silence, a rarity Harlan could not remember ever happening before the subject of college came up. He had read stories about families torn apart and those stories had always scared and confused him. Yet now, here he was living it.

"Uncle Harlan, I need to ask you a favor," Carly said. He looked up from his plate, surprised.

"What do you need, baby?"

"I know you don't approve. I know you don't understand. But I need you to try. I need to know you support me and still love me."

He slammed his sandwich onto the plate with such force it fell apart. "Damn it, Carly. Can't I have one meal without you throwing this shit in my face?"

"Harlan, language!" Noreen said. He ignored her.

"You know how I feel. Why do you even bring it up?"

"Because I need you to understand, to tell me you believe in me," Carly said.

Harlan didn't notice the tears in her eyes. All he could see when he looked at her was the betrayal, the anger and the hostility of the past few weeks.

"Uncle Harlan?" she pleaded. "Please?"

He ignored her.

"Harlan, she's trying to talk to you," Noreen said. "Are you going to listen to her? Or are you just going to keep plugging up your ears?"

Harlan glared at his wife. "So what, now you're on her side?"

"It's not about sides, Uncle Harlan."

He abruptly rose, sending his chair crashing to the floor behind him. He didn't bother picking it up before bellowing, "No. It's about family! It's about this family and you're tearing us apart."

"Harlan Cotton, I will not have you raise your voice at my table anymore," Noreen said. But he didn't hear her.

He stormed from the house, slamming the screen door behind him. He stalked across the back yard and into the barn, the horses stirring as he snatched open the door. Viking neighed and shifted nervously in his stall. Harlan moved to calm him.

"It's okay, boy," he said, but he knew the horse was reacting as much to his anger as he was to the sudden intrusion into the barn.

He tried to soothe him with a fist full of oats. As Viking nibbled from his hand, Harlan tried to focus his attention on the horse. The warm breath on his fingertips tickled and he began to feel the tension trickle through his neck and down his back. Viking finished the oats and Harlan unlatched the stall door. He led Viking out into the corral and was watching the horse trot laps when Carly climbed the fence beside him.

She rested her head on his shoulder and slid her arm into his. "I don't want to fight anymore, Uncle Harlan."

He kissed the top of her head. "I really don't understand. You've always loved it here. What has happened since the days when you argued with your mom about moving to Florida?"

She stared past the corral, across the pasture. "I don't know. A lot, I guess. I grew up and Casey and I... well, we always planned on college after he came back from the war. But that all changed, didn't it?"

He could not disagree. "But why leave? You have a life here. Friends, family. A support structure."

"And a whole world out there," she said. She nodded to the horizon. "A lot of world. And it's not like Austin is that far way."

"But what happens after Austin?" he asked. His phone rang and he looked down to check the I.D. The mayor was calling. It was the first time since well before Casey went off to war he had felt this close to Carly and the interruption would have to wait. He silenced the call.

"Well, after Austin," she began, but the phone rang again and she stopped. "Go ahead and answer it."

He sighed. "Yeah, Shep. What's up?"

"Harlan, I need you to come down to the office if you got a minute," the mayor said. His voice seemed more strained than usual. "There's been a development with Joe."

"Can it wait?" Harlan asked.

"I'm afraid not," Shep said.

Harlan turned to Carly, cupping his hand over the phone. "It's the mayor. Something's up downtown. Care to take a ride?"

She nodded. "That'll be nice."

Harlan returned to the phone. "I'll be right down, Shep."

Chapter Twenty–One

In the truck on the way to city hall a few minutes later, Harlan turned to Carly. "It's not that I don't want you to go to school. Or even to Austin."

"I know."

"I just don't want you to make a mistake and waste your time on something so frivolous," he said. She sighed.

"That's just the thing, Uncle Harlan. I don't think it's frivolous at all. It's important and it gives me meaning and comfort," she said.

"But are you sure? I mean really sure?"

She stared out the window. "Is anybody ever sure?"

"Damn it, yes. I was sure about my life," he said.

She turned sideways in the seat to face him. "Yes. Your life. You married the love of your life and took over the family farm. Then you got to retire early and play with me and horses. And I'm thankful for that, I so am. But I don't have that option. What do I have?" she asked, her voice pleading.

"Carly–"

"No, really. What do I have here? You and Aunt Noreen and a dead-end job at a diner? That's not a life. That's not a future. I want more. And I just figured eventually you'd understand that," she said.

Harlan pulled the truck up to the curb outside town hall and put it in park. "I do understand that, Carly. But you're so young."

"But I'm not stupid. And I'm not that young. I'm twenty. Everyone else I graduated with is either married or moved. There's no one here for me," she said.

"I'm here for you."

She turned away from him. "That's not what I meant."

Harlan knew he was losing, but he could at least make one attempt to salvage the day. "Do this for me, then."

She didn't turn away from window. "What?"

"If you'll spend two years taking classes at the community college, I'll give you my blessing. I'll even pay for UT," he said. It was a good offer and he knew she would have to consider it. "You won't have to move away immediately. And you can continue to save money. Then, if you decide to go on to art school, you won't have to work your way through. Fair enough?"

Carly was still staring out the window. Her shoulders slumped and she hung her head. "Fine."

Harlan leaned over and hugged her. "See, it all works out for the best."

Carly looked at her uncle and smiled. "If that's what it takes to make you understand, then fine. I'll do it."

"Good," he said. He looked out the window and saw the mayor waiting at the door. "I need to go talk to Shep. I'll be right back, okay?"

She nodded, silently.

Harlan stepped down from the Chevy and hurried to the waiting mayor, a youthful joy in his step that had been absent for a long time. Carly wasn't leaving and, as Harlan reached to shake the mayor's outstretched hand, he did not think there was a thing in the world that could kill his mood. "What's so important, Shep?"

"You remember Joey Caldwell and Carl Harding?"

Harlan thought for a minute. "Yeah. The two kids at the water tower?"

"Yeah. Well, they've made their usual trip up. You need to hear what they have to say," Shep said. "Then tell me what you think."

Shep led Harlan into his office, where the two boys were sitting in opposite chairs drinking soda. "Boys, you remember Mr. Cotton?"

They both nodded adding, in unison, "Yessir."

"Well, tell him what you told me."

Carl Harding looked up at the mayor. "Which part?"

"Start from the beginning," Shep said.

The boy glanced at his friend. Harlan could tell they were nervous. It wasn't every high schooler who wound up in the mayor's office to be interrogated. He definitely understood Carl's nervousness.

"Don't worry, son. You're not in trouble," Harlan said, trying to put the boy at ease. "So what you got for me?"

The boys took turns, nervously recounting their first trip up the tower, the web of metal stretching out across the roof. They told him about the second trip and the rolls of sheet metal they had seen and how those rolls disappeared bit by bit each time they climbed up for a look. But they could never quite see what it was the metal was being used for because it was obstructed from view. When they got to the last trip up the tower, earlier that morning, the boys both stopped and glanced at one another.

"Go ahead and tell him," Shep said.

"Well, we didn't see anything," Carl said.

"What? It was all gone?" Harlan asked. The boy shook his head.

"No sir," Joey Caldwell said. "We couldn't see because the roof was covered with a tent."

Chapter Twenty–Two

Before dawn on the morning of the fourth of July, Carly Machen declared her independence.

She arose well before sunup, her brain burning with a nervous energy. She looked at the suitcase on the floor of her bedroom, packed neatly with socks, her toothbrush, a few changes of clothes. Everything she would need for a few weeks in her new home fit neatly into a single bag at the foot of her bed. For a moment, she wavered, unsure if she would be able to go through with it. But she shook off her fear and sat down at her kitchen table, pen and paper in hand. She wrote a note to Doris and a resignation letter to Jimmy, folded them separately, and addressed each of them before placing both letters into a single envelope. She took the suitcase from her bedroom and placed it gently into the trunk of Casey's Mustang and, under the cover of darkness, drove across town to Doris Greely's house, where again she considered calling the whole thing off and returning to the comfort and security of her apartment and her bed. But something inside of her told her what she needed to hear. That apartment wasn't home anymore. Home was something she would have to make in Austin.

She slipped the envelope containing the two letters beneath the windshield wiper of Doris's car and rushed back to the Mustang still idling in the street. She took one good look at Doris's house before slamming the door and punching the accelerator without looking back.

Doris awoke a couple of hours later and found the envelope. But she didn't need to open it to know what was inside of it. As she read Carly's note, Doris thought about the times she had spent with the girl, how she had watched her grow up and how Carly was about to embark on the biggest adventure of her life. She read the brief letter thanking her for all she had done and inviting her to Austin, "whenever I get settled in," and she smiled to herself.

"You go, girl," she said to herself as she started her car and headed to the diner.

That morning, Harlan did not show up for breakfast. He wasn't at lunch, either. Doris began to get worried about him and considered calling Noreen but didn't. Instead, she resolved to seek him out at the fireworks that evening. Even though his niece was gone, Doris knew he would be somewhere on the town square, watching the festivities.

"Hey, Doris, how you feel if we close up shop early today," Jimmy asked her about three in the afternoon. "Since it's fireworks and all, I don't suspect we'll be having too many customers tonight."

"Fine by me," she said. "I was about to suggest the same thing."

"You wanna go together?" he asked. She shook her head.

"Nah, I wanted to check on Harlan before tonight. Carly leaving will just about kill him," she said. "As a matter of fact, would you mind if I cut out now?"

He shook his head. "Go on. I'll keep a watch on the place."

She untied her apron and tossed it onto the counter. At the door, she smiled. "We'll get through this, you and me."

He laughed. "Yes, we will."

She drove out to the Cotton place without bothering to stop and change. But Harlan was nowhere to be found. She sighed, checked her watch. It wasn't quite half past three and the Fourth festivities would not begin until closer to sunset.

"Well, Doris," she said to herself. "We'll just have to see him there after all."

She napped away part of the afternoon and almost missed the show. Doris arrived at the town square so late she was barely out of her car in time to see the first mortar fired into the sky over the bandstand. It burst, sending a shower of red, white and blue streamers spidering down. The crowd gasped, then clapped. With the second mortar, the music began. The crowd cheered. Doris searched the faces for Harlan or Noreen, but she couldn't find them. Nor did she see Shep or the Franklin brothers. In fact, there were so many people crammed into the square she couldn't pick out a single face. It was as if the whole of east Texas had merged into one collective mass, staring up at the heavens as twenty thousand dollars went, quite literally, up in smoke.

"Isn't it amazing?" she heard a voice say. "All this for our nation's birthday!"

Margie could barely contain her excitement, which made Doris giggle. Even she began to get caught up in the euphoria. Mortars and sparklers and streamers fired off in perfect time with the rising and falling notes of Tchaikovsky's overture. The sky became so filled with explosions, Doris could have read a book by the light cast down onto the townsfolk gathered below.

Children and parents stared up, agog. At each pause, they cheered. When the show continued, they cheered again. Doris's ears were ringing with explosions and shouts of glee as she glanced over to the Creedmore Building, where she almost expected to see Joe Morton standing on the roof, conducting his masterpiece. He wasn't there. But she did see Téo Barros standing on the corner, hugging a streetlamp and staring into the night sky.

She leaned over to Margie and tapped her on the shoulder. "You know, I wasn't expecting all this."

Margie nodded. "It's huge! Bigger and better than ever."

It was, Doris knew. In previous years, the display would have long been over. But here, now, because of Joe Morton's generosity, they were all still standing there, staring into the summer night, when the most familiar passages of the overture began. The pace of the sky bursts picked up in tempo with the music and, as the sky became increasingly filled with color and smoke and lights, the people of Cranston, Texas, fell silent in awe. Like everyone else there, Doris had listened to the 1812 Overture so many times in the past two weeks, she had committed the music to heart and was anxiously awaiting the cannon bursts. She wasn't disappointed.

The fireworks crew timed the launches perfectly so that each blast resulted in a spectacular, multi-staged explosion in the clear, deep black of the sky. At last, the trumpet fanfare came. The bells chimed, and the march began. The sky went mad. Hundreds of colors filled her entire field of vision until, at the very last, with the climax cacophony of music and light and sound, the sky went dark.

The crowd applauded loudly, shouts of "bravo!" and "way to go!" filling the air. Then, almost in unison, the entire crowd turned to the Creedmore Building, chanting for Joe Morton. The lights atop the building went dark and everyone gasped as a large, dark form ascended above the building with a loud clatter and locked into place above the roof.

"What the hell is–" Margie began, but she was interrupted by an unearthly hum and a blazing light.

The people all looked to the source of the light atop the Creedmore Building, a collective shock spreading across their faces. For there, wrought by sheer will from iron and aluminum and lights, towering to the heavens above Town Square, was Joe Morton's response to the good people of Cranston. His answer to the funeral, to Casey's death, to everything that had happened to him and around him. For all the things they had said and done, Joe had written them a message in seven, forty-foot tall, red-white-and-blue block letters.

FUCK YOU

The citizens of Cranston gazed up in stunned silence, unable to comprehend what they were seeing, as if they knew the sign was a hallucination or a dream brought on by the combined consumption of too many hotdogs and inhalation of too much smoke. Where only seconds before the sticky night air had been filled with the crashing rockets and the blaring, soaring finale of a Tchaikovsky masterpiece, it was now silent, penetrated by only one small noise. Somewhere near the back of the crowd, Doris Greely was laughing.

July: Joe Morton

Chapter Twenty–Three

The Monday following the Fourth of July, Jimmy asked Doris to tape a sign to the door of the Truck Stop Café before driving into Palestine for Joe's hearing in the district court there. The sign she hung read identically to the one the druggist hung on the door to the pharmacy and the one across town at the service station. In simple, handwritten letters on every door of every business in Cranston, were the words "Closed for Court."

In all the movies Doris had seen, the courtroom was divided down the middle, with victims or their families sitting behind the prosecutor's table and supporters of the defendant filling the benches behind the defense table. Her first experience in a courtroom, however, shattered that illusion. From her perch in the far back corner, Doris wondered how so many people could cram into so small a space. From the quiet murmurs, she deduced everyone was mad about Joe's sign. Occasionally, she could single out a voice over the hum. "Just you wait," one person would start before she'd lose the conversation. "…Sinful. It's sinful," another voice said.

At the front of the gallery, Harlan, Ted Bartley and the mayor were all huddled with Earl Meyers, the town's attorney. Earl had held the post since returning from World War II and, for a moment, Doris was somewhat surprised, as she was sure she had attended his funeral some years before. Nevertheless, there he was, leaning on the rail for support and cupping a hand to a withered ear in an effort to hear whatever Harlan and Shep were saying over the crowd.

Across the aisle at the other table sat Joe Morton. Vítor Barros was seated in the gallery, immediately behind him, with Téo at his side. Doris could only imagine what Joe was feeling in that moment, knowing that hundreds of sets of eyes were trained on the back of his head and that all the mumbling was about him. However, Joe turned around to say something to Vítor and changed her mind. He was smiling.

Though Doris knew Joe was destined to lose the hearing today, she was happy to see him smiling and laughing. All weekend, the talk at the diner had centered around whether or not they should file criminal charges. Harlan was out for blood and, Doris gathered, had the law on his side. This morning, this hearing, was the moment of truth for Joe and, by extension, for Vítor Barros.

The bailiff stepped forward, cleared his throat. "In the matter of the town of Cranston versus Joseph Morton, the honorable J. Lee Stephens presiding. All rise."

"Be seated," Stephens said, absently settling into the chair and opening the folder before him with a sigh. When the judge looked up at Joe, Doris almost expected him to laugh. "What the hell were you thinking, brother?"

"Judge, I thought that would be one thing that was pretty clear," Joe said with a grin. Most of the people gasped. A few chuckled.

The judge banged his gavel. "Order–and while I'm at it–this'll be the last interruption I'll tolerate."

The crowd fell silent and the judge nodded. "Much better. Now Joe, this is a serious matter. But I'll get back to that in a minute. Earl, what's the city's position?"

The old lawyer stood and removed his bifocals. "Your honor, this is a most egregious offense. What Joe has done is outright offensive to every man, woman and child living in the town of Cranston. Not to mention he's violated about nineteen statutes, including–"

"I got the brief, Counselor. We can save time and assume I know how to read," the judge said. "Joe, brother. Do you get how serious this matter is?"

"Yes, I do, Judge. I would ask if anyone else here does," Joe said.

Stephens sat up. "What do you mean by that?"

"Well, your honor, how many of these people have thought about how we got here in the first place?"

"Objection, your honor! Mr. Morton should not be able to drag the memory of his son into–"

But Stephens waved him off. "You don't even want to go there with me, Earl. You lot are the last people that get to talk to me about dragging that poor boy's memory anywhere."

Doris almost applauded, her heart racing. There on the bench sat a man who was able to say all the things she had not been able to say, everything she had been thinking but was unable to find the courage to speak. Earl slumped back into his chair. From the back of the courtroom, Doris couldn't help but feel optimistic for Joe's position.

Judge Stephens flipped a couple of more pages in the file, then looked back up at Joe. "Says here you ain't got an attorney, Joe."

"Don't much feel like I need one, Judge," he replied.

"Well, you're wrong. You need an attorney. It ain't my place to tell you that, but I'm telling you anyway. This ain't a laughing matter. But that's okay because you got at least one friend in the court today," he said. He craned his neck to see out into the gallery. "Melissa Cash Cavanaugh, approach the bench."

Every head turned to the rear of the courtroom, where a woman rose, statuesque above the gallery. The beat of her heels cut time as she made her way up to the bench. She paused long enough to smile at Joe before continuing forward.

Earl stood again. "Your honor, this is most unusual," he said, but Stephens just ignored him.

"Miss Cavanaugh, welcome to Palestine."

"Thank you, your honor."

"Excuse me, judge, but who is this?" a voice came from the gallery. Harlan was standing over Shep's shoulder, a look of confusion on his face. "We haven't heard of a Melissa Cash Cava–whatever."

The judge dropped the gavel to silence the crowd again. "I'm sorry, Harlan. Maybe I should introduce the two of you. Or maybe you should sit down before I throw you in the lockup for contempt. Your choice."

Harlan slouched back down into his seat, Stephens glaring at him the whole time. "As I was about to tell Joe, Miss Cavanaugh is down from Dallas. She's with a group who specializes in representing war protesters. And Joe, she's filed a letter to be added as counsel pro bono. That means she wants to be your attorney–for free."

Joe nodded. "I know what it means, your honor."

"Well, how do you feel about that?"

He shrugged. "Can't say I have much of an opinion either way, judge."

"Well, Miss Cavanaugh. That's good enough for me. Welcome to the case," Stephens said.

"Thank you, your honor," she said. She took a seat at the defense table beside Joe.

"Earl, you filed two motions. One is for an injunction against further display of the offending sign and the other is for summary judgment. Is that correct?"

"Yes, your honor. It's very obvious the defendant's actions are–"

"Earl, you can't have summary judgment in a criminal matter," the judge said. "There's that little matter about the Constitution and a trial by jury."

This time, a few more people joined in chuckling. Doris braced for the banging gavel but was surprised to see the judge smiling along with them. He looked at the bailiff, shaking his head.

"Miss Cavanaugh, what do you have to say about all this?"

She stood, a folder in her hand. "Your honor, while we understand the town's position, the defendant believes there are obvious constitutional questions. Luckily, those questions were settled in 1971. Cohen v California, in which the Supreme Court ruled the simple display of an expletive is not sufficient grounds for public obscenity."

She offered a folder to the bailiff, who passed it to the judge. "We've prepared a motion for dismissal on the grounds that Mr. Morton's actions are protected speech."

The judge skimmed the letter. "Figured as much." He turned to Earl. "What do you have to say about all this?"

"Well, I...I don't know."

The woman picked up where she left off.

"Your Honor, the Court ruled in '71 that, unless the object of the verb is something with which one can reasonably be expected to copulate, then–"

"I'm familiar with the case, Miss Cavanaugh. And while I have concerns about the sign, I have to agree with your application of the precedent to Mr. Morton's situation," the judge said. "So Earl, unless you've got something to add?"

Earl shook his head, silently.

"Well then, I'm dismissing all charges with prejudice. Court's adjourned." He slammed the gavel down.

Harlan jumped up. "Lee! You wait just a minute. What the hell does this mean?"

But J. Lee Stephens didn't stop. He kept on walking, the door to his chambers closing behind him. As the gallery filed from the courtroom, Doris could hear Harlan, pressing Earl. "I don't understand. What does that mean?"

"Stuff it, already, Harlan," Earl said. "It means we lost."

Chapter Twenty–Four

At the Café the next morning Doris was surprised when the first patron to step through the doors wasn't Harlan but was instead Joe's new lawyer. In one hand, the woman held her cell phone and car keys. The other was wrapped firmly around the handle of her smart, sleek attaché. She stood in the doorway a moment, as if she were surveying the Café for some missing detail. Finally, her eyes found Doris behind the counter.

"Just me," she said.

"Pick a seat, sweetheart. I'll be right with you."

Doris watched as the woman made her way to the back table–Harlan's table–and tucked herself into the booth. Doris almost said something to her but decided to allow events to unfold as they would. "What can I get you?"

"I suppose a cappuccino is out of the question?"

Doris smirked.

"I figured as much. How's the coffee?"

"Brown."

"Sounds great," she said. "Guess I'll have a coffee."

Doris righted the cup on her table and poured, taking in the imposing figure sitting before her. The woman, well, not much more than a girl, really, was taller than she remembered from the courtroom. Her chestnut hair was as tailored as her suit and fell around her face, flowing down over her shoulders and framing distinguished cheeks and a pair of piercing blue eyes. The woman smiled.

"You were in the courtroom the other day, yes?"

"Good memory."

"Not really. Just assumed. I think everyone was." She extended her hand. "Cash Cavanaugh. And you must be Doris?"

Doris stepped back. "Yes?"

"Joe told me about you."

Doris tried not to blush but failed. She drew her hand up nervously to brush her hair off her ear. "Well, really? I mean... what did he say?"

Cash smiled. "So what's the specialty here?"

"You like omelets? Can't beat Jimmy's ham and cheese."

She shook her head. "Sorry. Pescitarian."

"Peska-what?"

"I only eat fish."

"One of those. Scrambled eggs okay? Toast and maybe some grits?" Doris didn't wait for her customer to respond before writing out the ticket.

Cash's ears perked and she smiled. "I haven't had grits since I was a little girl. My grandmother used to fix grits. Thanks, Doris."

Rounding the counter, Doris dropped the ticket in the window and rang the bell. "Order in."

She watched as Cash opened her attaché and began removing folders. A notepad went on top of the stack with a gold-tipped fountain pen open across the top. Cash fished a small earpiece from her purse and fit it neatly behind her ear with her left hand as she pressed buttons on her cellular phone with the other.

"Sarah, it's Cash. Listen, I'm in Cranston...No, I think I'm going to stay for a few days. We won yesterday, but there's more going on here...Yeah, it's the one that just writes itself...Listen, I need a couple of things. Get in touch with the national office and tell them what's going on. I'll send you a picture in a few minutes to distribute to the usual suspects. I don't think this story's going away quite yet…Just a feeling I have."

She glanced up from her notepad and smiled at Doris before lowering her voice.

"You won't believe this place when you get here…I mean, Barney Fife, where are you?…I know, right? Maybe we can get that war mom down here? What's her name…yeah. That one…Check your mail in about three, babe."

When Cash closed the phone and tossed it back into her briefcase, Doris had to fight the urge to slap her. Instead, she would just give her a piece of her mind. Cranston was a small town and she didn't know from cappuccinos, but that didn't mean this woman, this stranger, was any better than her or Joe or even Harlan.

Jimmy rang the bell and passed Cash's plate through the window. "Order up!"

Saved by the bell, Doris thought. She consciously avoided the coffee pot, knowing Cash would need a refresher. Maybe if she made her wait–

"Would you freshen up my cup when you come?" Cash said. She smiled at Doris over the black rims of the glasses teetering on the end of her nose. "I'm afraid it's gone cold."

In the few seconds it took Doris to arrive at the table, Cash had deposited the folders into her briefcase and removed a laptop and small camera. She fumbled to plug a mouse into the side of the laptop, clicked a few times, then turned to Doris, a look somewhere between surprise and shock on her face.

"You don't have Wi-Fi."

"What are you babbling about now, child?"

"Internet. You don't have Internet?"

"Sure I got Internet. At home. Why on earth would I need it in a diner?"

Cash slammed the laptop. "I just don't…there's a whole world out there and you people exist outside of it!"

Doris rolled her eyes and dropped the plate on the table beside Cash's laptop. By then, Doris realized the woman wasn't any more interested in scrambled eggs than she was Joe Morton.

If eggs and grits were a means of feeding Cash Cavanaugh's stomach, Joe simply fed her superiority.

"Miss Cavanaugh, do you mind if I ask you a question?"

The woman looked up, again over the rim of her glasses. "Certainly not, Doris. And I told you, call me Cash."

"Why are you here?"

Cash cocked her head to one side. "Excuse me?"

"You ain't got a dog in this hunt. So why come down here?"

Cash smiled, removed her glasses, and leaned back, nodding. "I'm not going to give you the stock answer. You know I'd just say something trite. Like Joe needs my help. But that's not it, is it?"

Doris shook her head.

"So let's just talk. Come sit down with me for a second?"

"I can't–"

"Doris, there's no one here but us chickens and the cook. I don't bite."

"You sure about that?"

Cash winked. "Relax, Doris. I'm not going to hurt anybody."

As she sat down with her customer in Harlan's booth, Doris wasn't so sure. Everything about Cash Cavanaugh dripped poise and purpose. Suddenly, it all clicked in her head and Doris realized Cash for what she was, and then she smiled. Reaching across the table, she took Cash's hand and squeezed it. For the first time since Melissa Cash Cavanaugh glided through the courtroom and into their universe, the woman registered surprise. "I get it now."

Cash raised a quizzical eyebrow. "Get what?"

"Where you from, sweetheart?"

Cash started to answer, but Doris stopped her.

"I know you're down from Dallas. But where are you from?"

Before Cash could answer, the bells rattled against the glass and Doris turned to find Harlan standing at the door, staring at his table and the two women sitting there. She hustled to her feet and behind the counter.

"We'll get back to you later, sweetie," Doris said to Cash. She placed Harlan's mug on the counter and filled it. When he didn't make a move for it, she slid it a little further towards the edge.

"Just have a seat and I'll be right with you," she said, proud of herself that she got the sentence out without laughing. Harlan took the cup and started for a booth at the opposite end of the diner, stopping periodically to toss a curious, confused glance at the woman in his seat.

Doris made a cursory pass over Cash's table with the coffee pot. Cash had placed an American Express card on the corner of the table. Doris slid the card back towards her and leaned in close enough to whisper in her ear. "Breakfast is on me, doll."

Cash looked up quizzically, then followed Doris's gaze to the opposite end of the room, where Harlan was sitting, the same, befuddled stare written across his face. Doris winked at the woman and patted her shoulder. "Yep. That right there is worth breakfast. How long did you say you're in town for?"

"I don't know. Why?"

Doris did not answer. Instead, she just sauntered away, humming. A few minutes later, Cash Cavanaugh gathered her belongings into her briefcase and left. When Doris returned to the table, she found a twenty tucked beneath the coffee cup.

Chapter Twenty–Five

The sun beat down, baking the asphalt and sending a shimmering mirage into the air up the road from the barbershop. Harlan watched as a pair of mockingbirds fought over a scrap of paper on the bandstand in the square. He wasn't listening to whatever Ted Bartley was droning on about. It was just too hot to listen, watch the mockingbirds and ignore the cell phone buzzing in his pocket all at once. He did not recognize the number and silenced it.

The mockingbirds each seemed intent on ending up with the paper, though what the victor intended to do with it once he had vanquished his lesser, Harlan hadn't a clue. The first mockingbird, the smaller one, snatched the paper and made a mad dash around the bandstand but ducked back inside, close enough to the other, larger bird to allow a grab at the corner, which threw off the smaller bird. He lost both the paper and his equilibrium but quickly recovered and was again on the scrap, but could not seem to wrestle it free from the larger mockingbird. Just as it looked as if the larger of the two birds was about to win the battle, a gust of wind snatched it from both of them and carried it out onto the lawn, apparently farther than either bird was prepared to go for victory. And with that, the two birds jetted off in opposite directions.

Harlan chuckled. "Who does that woman think she is anyway?"

"Who?" Ted asked, apparently unaware that Harlan had not been listening.

"That bitch attorney. Coming up here and telling us what we can and can't do," he said. His temples began to pound and he could hear Noreen telling him to calm down before he had a heart attack or did something he'd regret. He took a breath before continuing. "I mean, what do we need with Hi-Wi or Wi-whatever? I've lived my whole life without e-mail and I'll do just fine without it now."

"You said the same thing about cell phones," Ted said. He laughed when Harlan's cell phone began to ring again.

Harlan didn't laugh. Instead, he silenced the call again. "What? So you're on her side?"

Neither man bothered to look up to so much as glance at what it was her side stood for. They didn't have to. Its shadow fell across the sidewalk, bathing half of Main Street in angular shadows.

"Earl says we could appeal but that it would cost too much money and the town's broke right now," Harlan said.

"Broke?"

Harlan nodded. "Casey's funeral. How's that for irony?"

Harlan's phone buzzed the announcement of waiting voicemail. Before he could check it, though, a rumbling truck interrupted the two men. They looked up the street and saw what looked like a large R.V. with a satellite dish attached to the top. It was windowless, save for the windshield and doors. As it rolled by and they saw the swooping CNN logo on the side, their hearts sank.

"Must have gotten lost on the way to Austin," Harlan said, so matter of factly, even he didn't believe himself.

Only a few seconds behind it came the second satellite van, the black "ABC" logo embossed into the sheet metal. The ABC van slowed down and Harlan and Ted watched as the driver leaned across the passenger to get a better look at Joe's sign.

Harlan stood to leave.

"This has gone too far," he said. Ted grabbed his wrist.

"What are you going to do?"

Harlan groaned. "Relax, Ted. I ain't going to kill her. Come on if you're that worried."

They piled into his truck and sped off after the news vans towards the Café. They caught up with the news vans and for a moment considered passing them, but didn't have to. The drivers pulled off at the motel. Five minutes later, Harlan and Ted stepped into the Truck Stop Café and made a beeline for the bar and Cash Cavanaugh.

"Miss Cavanaugh," Harlan said. She threw up a dismissive hand.

"Just a sec, Harlan. Finishing up a cappuccino for Doris," she said.

She emptied the contents of a packet into a cup of water and stirred it. "Whipped cream?" she asked. Doris passed her the can. She filled the cup the rest of the way up with the cream and passed the cup to Doris.

"It's not the same as a fresh one, but it's good enough to give you the idea," Cash said.

"Miss Cavanaugh–"

"I'll be with you in a minute," she said. "I don't want to miss this."

She watched as Doris sniffed the cup before taking her first sip. She winced, then smiled and took another sip. "It's different."

Cash beamed. "But you like it, don't you?"

Doris nodded and wandered off with the cup. Cash reached into her purse and began making a second cup for herself. "Want one, boys? I have plenty."

Harlan pushed the cup away. "We don't need your fancy-assed coffee here," he said.

Cash sighed and turned to face him. "This is about Joe's sign, isn't it?"

"No, it's about you," Harlan said. "Coming up in here with your laptops and your briefcases and your cappuccinos and trying to change us. Where do you get off?"

Cash scoffed and shrugged. "I just...Harlan, you can't keep the world out forever."

Harlan flushed and his pulse quickened. "I ain't concerned about the world. What I want to know is why A, B, fucking C is parked at the motel!"

Cash smiled, sipped her cappuccino and looked up at him, calmly. "Because I called them."

Harlan opened his mouth to respond, but instead, froze when he noticed the television in the corner. It was tuned to CNN, and there on the screen, a reporter was standing in front of the Creedmore Building.

"Turn that up, will you, Jimmy?" he said.

Without a word, Jimmy upped the volume. For one moment, Harlan and Doris both waited, hoping this was all a bad dream. But as the volume came up, Doris knew it wasn't.

She shook her head. "Oh my God."

"...in downtown Cranston, Texas, where one man has lodged his formal complaint against the war effort," the reporter said. "You've heard of the war mom? Well try this one on: the War Dad."

Doris turned to Harlan, but he was already out the door and into his truck. The silver truck peeled out of the parking lot and onto the highway in a cloud of smoke. She turned back to the television.

"We can't show you the whole sign because of FCC regulations. You'll just have to trust us when we say it's there. The F-bomb. And the word you, in forty-foot-tall red white and blue," the reporter said.

111

The camera panned across a growing crowd in the barely recognizable Cranston town square. Doris recognized few of the faces milling about as the reporter narrated the growing scene, with blankets and tents and more than one person playing anti-war tunes on a guitar.

Finally, the camera settled back on the reporter. "I'm joined now by Marjorie Bartley, the proprietor of one of the many mom-and-pops in Cranston. Mrs. Bartley, what do you think of the latest addition to the Cranston skyline?"

She hoped she had heard wrong. Yes, that must be it. But, as the camera panned to take in the guest, Doris swallowed hard. "Oh dear God."

"What do I think?" Margie said to the reporter. She shifted nervously, glanced at the camera. "Well, it's just. I mean, look at it, at all the people. It's really unfortunate about his son and all–"

"Joe Morton's son, yes?"

Margie nodded. "I understand he lost a son and all. But, when you look around and see what this is turning into, well. It's just–"

"You run a motel here, right?"

"Yep. For twenty-eight years," Margie said. She added quickly, "Almost twenty-nine."

"And, with all the people coming into town, I would imagine this has been pretty good for business?" the reporter said.

"Well," Margie hesitated. "I guess. I mean, I haven't looked at it that way."

"Mrs. Bartley, there are people who are criticizing Mr. Morton for his sign. They say it's anti-American, unpatriotic. Do you agree?"

Margie seemed to eye the crowd for a moment, then turned her gaze upwards. Doris knew she was looking at the sign and she knew where this was headed. All Doris could do was shake her head.

"I mean, it's free speech and all," Margie said. "Joe Morton should get to say his piece, even if we don't like it. After all, Joe gave his son to this country and that makes him a patriot."

Doris turned off the television. She leaned across the counter, head in her hands, and cast a sidelong glance at Cash, who was still sitting at the bar sipping her cappuccino. "What now?"

"Now the world comes," Cash said.

Chapter Twenty–Six

Harlan lay, propped against a mountain of pillows, his hand fidgeting with the volume buttons on the remote control. He was not watching the news program on the screen, but he couldn't bear to turn it off. The television was the only distraction that successfully diverted his attention away from the voicemail from Waco. Even if the news was consumed with talk about Cranston, it still kept him from thinking about the phrases "rising PSA's" and "possible surgical remedies." Despite the need for the distraction of the television, though, Harlan could not bring himself to turn up the volume and listen to the commentary. He knew his blood pressure couldn't take the added stress. Besides, with the television muted, he could listen to his wife's phone call in the other room.

She was talking to Carly and, so far, Harlan had picked up a few choice details about his niece's adventures. School was going good. Had she met any boys? Well, one would come–eventually. No, Noreen understood if Carly wasn't quite ready for boys yet. Was the apartment nice? Was she eating enough? Maybe Noreen and Harlan could come down for a visit soon and bring her winter clothes.

Twice, Noreen appeared in the doorway and motioned to the phone, a silent suggestion that Harlan might want to speak to his niece.

Twice, he turned her down.

It was a step he simply wasn't ready for yet.

"No, sweetie, he's still in the bathroom," she said after the second offer.

The talking head on the T.V. was standing, "Via Satellite," on the Cranston Town Square. In the split screen, another talking head was from Washington. Occasionally, a third would appear from Los Angeles and, it was apparent, the two from Washington and Los Angeles were arguing about the sign and its true meaning.

Harlan knew because he had seen the original broadcast earlier in the evening and had turned it off when the man from Los Angeles began defending Joe Morton as an example of "a true patriot." Harlan simply wouldn't abide that kind of nonsense in his house and had turned it off before the conclusion of the program, despite Noreen's objections that she wanted to hear Margie's interview with "that Irish boy from New York. You know the one," she had said.

Noreen appeared in the doorway, smiling, the phone still pressed to her ear. "Okay, sweetheart. I'll be sure to tell him. Goodnight."

She tossed the cordless onto the bed next to Harlan and folded back the comforter. Sitting with her back to him, she heaved a sigh. "Carly says we're the talk of Austin. Joe's sign is all anybody can talk about."

When he didn't reply, Noreen prodded his shoulder. "You know you're eventually going to have to talk to her, right?"

He grunted but said nothing. He didn't know what to say. He just wanted to sleep, but Noreen very obviously had other plans.

"Really, Harlan. How long are you going to punish her?"

He turned off the set and removed his glasses. "Is that what you think this is? Punishing her?"

"Certainly what it seems."

She slid beneath the covers, rolled onto her side and reached to turn off the lamp, but stopped. Turning back to Harlan, she patted his chest. "She's been your baby girl since forever and now I can't bear you like this. She needs to know you still love her."

"I still love her just fine. It's just I've got so much to deal with." He pointed to the television. "Joe's little debacle's got us in a state, Noreen. Don't know if you've noticed or not, but up the road, CNN is waiting for your close-up. You really want to have to deal with this shit much longer?"

"Language, Harlan Cotton! And no, I don't want to have to deal with anything–which is precisely what you're doing. Or not."

"What's that supposed to mean?"

"You've not so much as spoken to the girl since she left. You think you're hurt? Imagine how she must feel."

Harlan rolled away from his wife in a huff. He knew she was right. But there was too much to do for him to worry about his wayward niece. Besides, hadn't she made her bed? She left. And now, here he was, stuck dealing with Joe Morton and the entirety of the national media piled up at the motel.

"I'm sorry," he said.

"For what?" Noreen replied without moving.

"For being mad. For everything. But I mean, you have to understand," he said.

"I do. But maybe you have to understand you can't control what Joe Morton does any more than you can control what time the sun comes up. Harlan, you're going to have to let go before you give yourself a stroke over this. Remember what you used to tell Carly when the kids were picking on her?"

"Ignore it–"

"–and it'll go away," she said, finishing his sentence. "Just ignore it all. It'll go away."

"This ain't kids picking on Carly, Noreen. The goddamned thing is forty feet tall and I'm pretty sure no amount of ignoring will make it go away."

"Again with the language. I'm going to throw you to the couch if you keep this up," she said. "And for the record, it was Carly who said ignore it, Harlan."

"That's the same thing Shep said earlier," Harlan said. "It'll blow over if we just let it. I just hope to hell they're right."

She kissed Harlan's forehead. "They are right. You should listen to them."

Chapter Twenty–Seven

Despite everyone's best assurances that the attention was only temporary, six days later the sign was still headlining news reports across the country. People kept coming and, when they got to the square, they stayed. Less than a week after the fireworks display, a transient community had formed, peopled by war protesters, gawkers and food vendors. Almost overnight, the citizens of Cranston were marginalized and, sitting on the bench outside the barbershop taking in the scene, Harlan decided he hated the hotdog vendors most of all.

"How d'you suppose they got here?" he mumbled.

Ted didn't look up from the Sun-Times when he answered. "Came in on a truck from Austin about two days ago."

Harlan spat onto the sidewalk. "Vultures."

"Hm?"

Harlan pointed to the vendor. "Damned hotdog vendors. Why'd they come, anyway? They think we didn't have food?"

"Free country, Harlan," Ted said. "Besides. The Café's been full for the week. Margie and I couldn't get a table this morning. Damnedest thing I've ever seen. You should see poor Doris, running around best she can since Carly left. Have you heard from her lately?"

Harlan shook his head. "Noreen talked to her last night. She's getting ready to start classes soon."

He was going to continue, but something at the Creedmore Building caught his eye. He watched as Joe's truck pulled to a stop at the curb. The driver's door opened and, instead of Joe, Harlan was surprised to see Vítor Barros exit and start towards the side door with a toolbox propped on his shoulder.

"Great. Now what the hell have they got going?"

Before Ted could respond, Harlan was off the bench and headed across the street. He managed to make it across the street and to the door before Vítor saw him. "Good morning, Mr. Cotton. How are you today?"

"Where's Joe?" he asked.

"I do not know. Would you mind opening the door for me? It should be unlocked," Vítor said. The toolbox rattled as he jostled it on his shoulder, trying to keep it balanced.

Harlan reached for the handle, but stopped. "Why don't you tell me what your game is here?"

"I'm sorry, Mr. Cotton. I assure you there is no game. I come for work, for Mr. Morton. That is all," he replied. He shifted the toolbox again. "Mr. Cotton, the door, please? We will talk more inside."

Harlan reluctantly opened the door, holding it open for the tall Brazilian, who ducked as he entered. Following him inside, Harlan studied the store to see if he could determine the nature of what had gone on inside. In spite of his closest observation, though, he couldn't find anything of interest in the entire building. No more secret projects. The space was empty, save a couple of old wooden crates left over from the furniture store days.

Vítor dropped the tools to the ground with a grunt. "Much better now. So, Mr. Cotton. You were asking about Mr. Morton. He is at home, working on his tractor. That is why I came into town–for my welding machine."

Harlan continued to study the room. There were tools strewn about and interweaving trails of footprints in the layer of fine dust covering the tile floor. He turned back to Vítor, who was kneeling at the toolbox, fishing a pipe wrench from beneath the mass of tools.

Something about the always formal tone in Vítor's voice set uncomfortably with Harlan, as if the accent were not enough to remind him this man was an alien. He looked again to the footprints in the floor for some clue to the question that was trying to form in his mind. Vítor responded before Harlan could ask.

"Forgive me, Mr. Cotton, but I must ask" Vítor said, glancing up. "Why do you dislike Mr. Joe so much?"

Vítor's question had come with the same ease he approached disconnecting the welding machine, but despite the Brazilian's tact, Harlan felt offended nonetheless and snapped, "I do not expect someone who is not from here to understand, Mr. Barros."

"You may have a point there," Barros said with a chuckle. He looked up from the valves of his welding gear, quizzically. "Perhaps you can explain something else to me, then. America is the land of free speech, yes?"

Harlan nodded. "That's right."

The valve on the tank broke free, and Vítor released a sigh and tossed the valve into his toolbox. Dusting his hands on his pants, he stood.

"So I'm confused, Mr. Cotton. Why is Mr. Joe's sign anything but patriotic?"

Harlan felt his ears turning red. "Excuse me? Who the hell do you think you are? This is America."

"Yes, Mr. Cotton, and a great nation as well. However, was it not your President Jefferson who said dissent is the purest form of patriotism?"

Harlan stepped forward, closing the distance between the pair too quickly. He expected Barros to step back, but the man didn't move, did not seem to register the move. Instead of flinching, Barros stood his ground, a gentle smile creeping across his face.

"Mr. Cotton, I have to be going. Mr. Morton is waiting."

Harlan stepped back. "Right. The tractor."

"Yes, the tractor."

Heading for the door, Harlan stopped. "I thought the Carmichael boy cut his pasture."

"Yes, he did, until the fireworks. His parents will no longer allow him to assist Mr. Morton," the Brazilian said. "Though speech is free, it is rarely without price. Don't you think?"

Chapter Twenty-Eight

Doris knew she should be in a hurry, but she had allowed the mellow, tinny music and crisp air from the open coolers to lull her into serenity. She had already gotten what she came for–eight dozen eggs and seven pounds of bacon–and now she was taking a leisurely pass down the baking aisle, pondering whether or not she wanted to make a cake in if so, whether she was in the mood for chocolate or strawberry.

For the third time since she left the diner, her cell phone buzzed in her pocket. She made no move to answer it because she knew it was Jimmy. And she knew he was calling to tell her to pick up several loaves of bread. It had become their morning routine over the past couple of weeks. She would rush out, leaving behind the new girl from Grapeland to tend the diner full of customers while she rushed to the market for whatever they had just run out of.

Doris steered the shopping cart around a corner in the general direction of the bakery without looking and almost rolled into Margie Barley. She shrieked, bringing the cart just shy of Margie's rear.

"Guess that's why women shouldn't be operating machinery," Doris said.

Margie laughed. "I see we're both out of things."

"Service truck runs once a week and, with all the people, can't seem to keep eggs around," she replied. "Ted told me you guys had to open up the back wing?"

"Full up. Would you believe some people are even sharing a room with strangers?"

"Tell the truth, I wouldn't know what to believe anymore," Doris said. Margie turned her cart alongside Doris's and the pair continued to the bakery. Doris shook her head in disbelief.

"Jimmy has called some company to come in and put wireless Internet at the diner. I got asked to make a latTé the other day. I didn't even know what a latTé was."

Margie chuckled. "Ted says we ought to offer room service 'cause people can't get into the diner. How's the new girl working out?"

Doris studied loaves of bread, pressing on the tops to test the firmness of each before selecting it for the cart. "She's okay. I mean, she ain't from around here so that's probably a good thing."

"How so?"

Doris stopped checking loaves. "Well, she don't know who all is from here and who ain't, so she treats everyone the same. Good for the visitors."

"And what about the regulars?"

It was Doris's turn to laugh now. There, between the wheat bread and hamburger buns, she lost it. "He came in this morning, couldn't get his seat. I thought he was going to throw things, Margie. I really did."

Margie grinned. "Ted says it's just awful all the people packed in. Of course, he ain't complaining about them packed in down at the motel. Says we may go to Hawaii for Christmas. Can you imagine? Me on a beach in Hawaii? Well, I'd better jet. Ted's waiting for the bleach for the linens."

Doris grabbed two extra loaves of wheat for good measure and, dropping them into her cart, headed for the checkout, almost unable to work through her exhaustion. She had lived in Cranston all of her life and worked at the Truck Stop Café since high school. For the most part, she had been pleased with her life until recently. But, with the lights of the world shining on her town, Doris found herself longing for that which she had never had and never really wanted–a vacation.

The checkout line didn't help her mood. Along both sides, magazine covers beamed with pictures of celebrities and politicians on beaches, at parties, generally in places Doris would never see. She chuckled at her own silliness, an effort to lift her mood. It worked until she got into the car and realized she had to go back to work.

Driving back to the diner, Doris allowed her mind to stray to the people that were there. Any time before Casey's death, she would have taken comfort in the familiar faces, the predictability of the regulars. She would have been able to write their orders and drop the ticket before they were even out of their cars. By the time her customers were to the door, she would have a steaming cup of coffee waiting on their table–with cream and sugar if they liked it. That mindless consistency had always been a comfort to her. Cash Cavanaugh and her litany of outsiders had brought something new to Doris's life. A disquiet followed her days and she wasn't sure that the underlying cause represented something altogether unpleasant.

Though she shared many of the same concerns, the same fears, as Harlan and the rest of her neighbors, Doris couldn't get past a sense of excitement when she saw Cash's rented Chrysler in the parking lot. Her pulse quickened when she heard the woman's distinctive laugh escape through the open door for just a second as a customer entered. And she could not help but smile as she saw Cash, leaning over the counter, trying to show the new girl from Grapeland how to work the cappuccino machine she'd had her assistant deliver from Dallas three days before.

And there, watching Cash fiddle with knobs, steam spewing out across the counter, Doris finally recognized the source of her restlessness. Before Joe's stunt, before the arrival of the lawyers and the T.V. vans and the protestors and the gawkers, Doris had never given much thought to the world outside of Cranston. Joe's sign struck some chord with the outside world and, as a result, the outside world came to Cranston. Stepping into the Café, Doris realized that the outsiders, with all of their allure, were striking their own chord. Their world was beckoning and Doris wondered for how long she would be able to ignore its call.

Chapter Twenty–Nine

Shep adjusted Frederick Gruber's nameplate for the third time before checking to make sure his wife had actually filled the water pitchers sitting between each of the seats. Closing the blinds on the windows to block out a late summer sun, Shep noticed storm clouds across the field and checked his watch, estimating how long it would be before the storm arrived. It was the first time in his twenty years as mayor of Cranston that he had ever moved a board of aldermen meeting from Town Hall and Shep wanted to make sure there was no room for complaints and no reason for anyone to claim they couldn't get in.

He stepped down from the stage and took several steps back into the cafeteria, among the rows of tables where, during the school year, a hundred elementary kids gathered to eat lunch. In little more than an hour, the people of his town would crowd into that same space for another opportunity to mingle with their visitors.

He studied the table to ensure everyone would be seated in their assigned spots. Frederick would be seated next to Ted Bartley. Shep himself would take the center seat, between Ernest Golson and Ted. And at the far end, Margie would occupy the final seat at the board table, the four aldermen and the mayor constituting the government of Cranston. To one side, as Shep had requested, a side table had been set up for Sheriff Tolar and

Earl. Cranston would need its legal team if it was going to keep order over the next few days.

Shep considered for a moment finding a microphone for that table, but he heard a bump behind him and turned to find the first visitor to the cafeteria. It wasn't Frederick or any of the other aldermen, but a photographer, dropping a case of equipment.

"Sorry," the man said. "This is where you want us, isn't it?"

Shep shrugged. He hadn't given a single thought to the media, but now that the photographer was locking a video camera onto his tripod, Shep realized just how different his world had become and the weight of this meeting began to press down upon his shoulders. This wasn't just about his constituents or the people camping out in the town square. It wasn't even about Joe Morton or his son anymore. Standing in the elementary school's cafeteria, Shep couldn't help but wonder what any of it was about anymore.

"It's just all so much bigger than us now," he said, more to himself than to his wife who had just walked up.

"You just do what you think's right and everyone will respect that," she said. He felt her fingers slipping into his and pulling him closer. "I've never been more proud of you than today."

She pulled his shoulder down and kissed his cheek. "This'll all work out. Just you watch."

She checked her watch. "Look at the time. I've got to run to the house."

"What for?" he asked.

She nodded to the photographer, fiddling with knobs on his camera. "I'm the mayor's wife. I have to look presentable. Don't worry. I'll be back in an hour."

Shep watched his wife leave and then did what he always did before the meetings. He mounted the stage, took his seat at the center of the table and fell asleep reading the agenda.

Frederick Gruber nudged him awake a half-hour later. For a moment he forgot where he was and smiled at his old friend.

Frederick's attention, however, remained fixed on the back of the room. "And you should see the parking lot."

Shep eyed the line of reporters along the back of the cafeteria across the crowd of people that had begun to gather. He recognized some of the faces from earlier broadcasts and noticed several new faces. In the crowd he had to search for the friendly faces of his neighbors. Aside from the occasional flash of familiarity, the entire room seemed filled with people he'd never met. Finally, near the exit, his eyes met sympathy. His wife was seated snuggly beside Noreen Cotton, clutching her arm in support. He smiled.

Ted leaned over and cupped his hand over the mayor's microphone. "You want to get started, Shep?"

Shep nodded and reached for the gavel, but a quick glance at the agenda made him stop. Instead, he cleared his throat to silence the audience.

"Ladies and gentlemen, if you'd bear with us for just a moment, it seems the first two speakers on our agenda are not here yet and–"

He was interrupted by a commotion from the hallway outside the cafeteria. He smiled. "And there they are. Sheriff, would you please inform Mr. Cotton and Miss Cavanaugh we're all waiting on them?"

The sheriff nodded to a deputy standing near the back door. While the crowd waited in silence, the deputy slipped into the hallway. A few moments later, he returned with Harlan and Cash in tow.

"Now then," Shep said, dropping the gavel. "I call this meeting of the Cranston Board of Aldermen to order. Everyone, please stand for the invocation and the pledge. Alderman Gruber, would you do the honors?"

Chapter Thirty

It was the tiniest dent in the seat bottom, not really even a dent so much as a bump, just perceptible enough to dig into her thigh. Cash Cavanaugh considered shifting her weight in the folding metal chair to alleviate the tingling sensations creeping down her left leg. But she had been at this game for more than a decade now and knew that the slightest hint of discomfort would be interpreted as a weakness. The aldermen hurling question after question at her might not even consciously register the shift. Nevertheless, even a flinch of less than an inch would chum the water and might quicken an attack that, as yet, had not come.

Thus she resolved not to relieve the pressure, to remain still, and just return to her seat very carefully once their questions had ended. Right now, they were busily discussing the need for security arrangements for the shops downtown, despite the hardware guy's insistence that such steps were unnecessary.

"Sheriff, we don't need extra security," Golson said. "In fact, I ain't sure you guys have more to worry about from our own people than the hippies."

A murmur moved through the crowd. Cash was pleased the turn was happening with so little effort on her part. She knew how the rest of the meeting would unfold. At the right moment, she would decide to speak.

Shep banged the gavel to silence the audience. "We ain't going to get out of hand here. And we're not to the part of the agenda to discuss security yet. So let's keep on topic, shall we?"

The four aldermen nodded their silent agreement and Shep eyed the audience again, a final assurance that they would remain silent and polite, before continuing. "Miss Cavanaugh, you were saying?"

"I was saying I cannot speak to the will of the people downtown. My involvement is only as Mr. Morton's lawyer, nothing more."

She knew it wasn't the answer he had wanted. They had asked her to come to tell them about war protesters and how to get rid of them or appease them. The aldermen represented the powers and the powers wanted to know how to restore order—order as defined narrowly by returning them to authority and life to the way they wanted it. But each subsequent murmur that moved across the crowd carried within it the seeds of realization that their town was forever, fundamentally different in some way and, despite their best machinations and wailings, would never be the same again.

"If that's the case, Miss Cavanaugh, then why are you still here?"

It was a simple enough question, and under the circumstances, she was surprised that Ted Bartley had managed to mask his hostility. She smiled at him and leaned forward to the microphone. "Alderman Bartley, I am representing my client in an ongoing legal dispute with the Town of Cranston. My contract with him extends until I'm convinced that all legal matters concerning his use of his private property downtown—"

"You mean the sign, right?" This time, the interruption came from Frederic Gruber.

"Yes, the sign. So long as there is a potential for legal action against my client because of that sign, I'll remain here until the window for appeals prescribes—." She glanced down at the notepad before her, though she knew the date by heart. "–this Thursday."

Golson cleared his throat. "Are we pursuing an appeal, Mayor?"

Cash noticed the mayor fidget with his pen for a moment before he turned to the town attorney. "Earl, what was your thought on an appeal?"

Earl heaved a sigh. "About a hundred thousand dollars, give or take."

Cash considered correcting what she knew to be an obscenely low estimate. A First Amendment challenge could easily run into millions and her backers had very deep pockets. Though she knew of several conservative groups that might back such a case, those groups steered more towards affirmative cases as well and probably wouldn't get involved against Joe's sign. No, Cash knew the sign was there to stay as long as Joe wanted it. In her younger days, she would have leaped in, thrown about numbers ranging from hundreds of thousands into the millions, but years of experience had tempered her. She knew leaving them to speculate would prove a far more effective means of preventing an appeal. Her work in Cranston done, she decided to let Earl's lowball estimate stand.

Shep let the aldermen discuss the figure for a moment before again clearing his throat. "I think, if the events of the past few weeks have shown us anything, it's that we can't afford any additional expenses."

Golson raised his hand. "Mayor, I for one don't think I'd support an appeal."

Cash fought the urge to smile or cheer. This was the moment she had been waiting for. A new wave of murmurs moved across the room. This time, Shep did nothing to stop it. Instead, he turned, stunned, his mouth open, as if he were about to speak. But it was another voice from the back of the room that gave the fullest meaning to Shep's stunned expression.

"What the hell?"

Everyone turned to find the speaker, though the residents of Cranston knew the voice and the face to whom it belonged. For there, in the back of the cafeteria, Harlan Cotton had bolted from his seat and was straining against Noreen's grip around his wrist.

At last, her victory all but assured, Cash shifted and allowed the blood to return to her left foot. Her backers would be pleased with the job she had done.

"Mayor," she said, "I believe I'm done here?"

Shep nodded. "Yes, Miss Cavanaugh, I believe you are."

Chapter Thirty–One

Harlan twisted his wrist against Noreen's grip, trying to pull away. He wasn't sure why she was holding him back in the first place. Did she think he was going to punch the attorney or commit some other, more heinous crime? He looked down and tugged again, but she growled.

"Harlan Cotton, you put your ass back in that seat. You're embarrassing me in front of my friends," she said through clenched teeth.

Harlan looked around the room, at the hundreds of eyes fixed on him. Shep's gavel was hanging in the air above the sound block and he was staring Harlan down into his seat. Even that attorney was eying him with those eyes, those too-inquisitive, accusing eyes. He could feel his blood pumping faster, the veins in his neck straining against the collar of his tee shirt. What did she have to blame him for? He wasn't the one who built the sign, who brought in that Mexican and sent Carly to Austin. And he most certainly wasn't the sand nigger that blew up the Morton boy's truck.

"Let me go, Noreen," he said.

She released her grip and he stormed from the cafeteria, the doors slamming behind him. In the parking lot, Harlan could see into the school through the windows to where the meeting had fallen into bedlam. Shep was banging the gavel and trying to quiet down the crowd, which had divided into two opposing sides, one filled with angry faces he recognized and one filled with angry hippies from the town square. Even the aldermen were yelling into their microphones, ignoring Shep's gavel. Harlan shook his head, climbed into the truck and left tracks in the parking lot, tearing onto the highway.

Harlan wasn't sure where he was going, but he had to get as far away from that school and those people, as fast as possible, and before the sea swell of emotions overtook him and he actually did do something he would regret. He floored the accelerator and the Silverado let loose a deep, throaty roar. As the speedometer climbed, Harlan pretended that, with enough speed, he could outrun it all. Joe's sign, the angry voices at the meeting, even the cancer vanished in the wake of dust the truck kicked up. Without looking away from the road, he turned on the radio and rolled down both windows.

The sudden burst of heat carried with it the sweet scent of ozone and the promise of a summer thunderstorm. Checking the rearview mirror, Harlan noticed occasional fingers of lightning snaking down through the sky to the south. The setting sun bathed the approaching clouds in orange-purple light. Still, it was an hour or so away, he figured. That left plenty of time for a drive. But the gas gauge wouldn't hold out for that kind of travel. So a quick detour to the gas station yielded a full tank, a bag of beef jerky, and a six-pack of Miller Genuine Draft. Harlan dropped the bag of jerky into his lap, popped the top on a beer, and headed back out onto the highway.

The road leading from the gas station ran in a perfectly straight line for thirty miles to the west before veering south into the next county at the foot of Harper's Hill, a modest rise in the terrain that the planners had opted not to go over or cut through. Instead of routing around the hill, the road took a dangerously hard turn to the left that sent it, inexplicably, to Austin. Over the years, that turn had claimed more than its fair share of long-haulers and drunken teens. Harlan always wondered why, during the planning stages of the highway, they hadn't simply adjusted the trajectory of the road a couple of degrees in order to avoid the hill altogether. He had seen it on the map, knew that adjusting the road just a few degrees to the east or west would have sent it straight into the next county and through half a dozen towns. Now, though, driving the highway in anger, Harlan was thankful. Harper's Hill would mark a good way-point for him to turn around and head home. He kicked back in the driver's seat and just sipped his beer, the hot Texas winds cutting through the cab of the truck and carrying with them all of the stress, the anger of the past few months, leaving behind only the fatigue of a well-fought, if lost, fight.

His mind clearing, Harlan began to think of all that had happened and wondered if he could have changed the outcomes. Carly wanted to go to art school. She went to art school. Joe wanted to build his sign. The sign was built. Harlan got cancer. The cancer spread. There wasn't a thing on earth Harlan could have done to change any of that and on some level he understood that. But did comprehension mean he had to accept the consequences? It wasn't like he always got his way. He was married, after all, and in all their years Noreen had won her fair share of fights.

He popped the cap off another beer. The land around him was starting its gradual rise and fall, marking the far edge of the county. The sun was setting behind Harper's Hill, casting deepening shadows in the pastures. He'd have to turn around soon. Harlan brought the truck to a stop at the foot of the hill, checked the curve, then pulled a U-turn.

The sun fell squarely in his rearview mirror and Harlan moved to adjust it. As he did, he saw the answer hanging on the rack in the back window. He opened the third beer and smiled. Maybe there was a way to rid Cranston of Joe Morton and his sign after all.

Thirty minutes and the three remaining Millers later, Harlan parked the Silverado beneath the water tower and slipped his dad's Winchester off the rack. He slung it over his shoulder, grabbed a handful of cartridges from beneath the seat and slammed the door. The sun had set. For the most part, Cranston was bedded down for the night. He could see only the top of Joe's sign from the ground. Harlan was surprised when it took him less than five minutes to climb the ladder to the catwalk at the top of the tower.

He eased down onto the catwalk, slipped the .308 off his shoulder and loaded the first round into the chamber with a sneer.

The first shot cut into the night and echoed through downtown. Later, people would remember where they were when they heard the first shot, even people who were too far away to have heard anything. People in the distance assumed it was thunder. Those too close to make such a mistake figured someone had finally caught the coon turning over the garbage. Gunshots weren't unheard of in the country. As loud, as unexpected, as frightening as the first shot was, it was the second shot that made people sit up and take notice. To Cranston natives, Harlan had decided to take back his town. But to the people crowded into the makeshift community on Town Square, the shot was an alarm that propelled them from their tents and back onto Main Street.

With his first two shots, Harlan had simply punched holes through the sign. It wasn't until he took aim for the third that he realized the perfect target. Raindrops were beginning to fall, so he'd have to work fast. He had no desire to end it all, the victim of a wet ladder.

He drew down on his target, a silver panel no bigger than a shoebox, tucked away neatly on a post between the F and the U. With the expert marksmanship of an Army man, he sighted in, held his breath, and squeezed the trigger.

The shot rang out into the night and was followed by a deafening silence. He thought for a moment he heard the collective gasp of the crowd as the sign went dark and he smiled to himself.

"How's that for a fuck you, Joe," he said aloud.

He slung the rifle back over his shoulder and began the trek down the ladder. The wind kicked up again and, as Harlan reached the ground, the fat, heavy drops of summer rain pelted his shirt. He slipped the rifle back into the rack, climbed into the Silverado and spun his tires in the gravel as he sped out onto the dark Cranston streets.

Chapter Thirty-Two

Shep pulled into Town Square and put the Buick into park. The windshield wipers flapping back and forth in the rain lent an artificial rhythm to the scene spread across the square before him. The masses of people he had expected to find nestled in their tents were crowded under the bandstand, huddled around trees or crouching beneath shared umbrellas. Shep was surprised when he recognized a few familiar faces among them. Two quick siren beeps and a flash of red drew Shep's attention to the sheriff's cruiser in his rearview. A poncho-clad Tolar slithered out of the cruiser. Shep reached for his umbrella but saw the drenched people in the square and returned the umbrella to the back seat. The rain was coming down pretty much sideways anyway.

"Evening, Mayor," the Sheriff said. "Sorry to bug you during the storm, but you'll just have to see this for yourself."

"What's happened?"

Sheriff shrugged. "We got reports of gunshots. Then when my deputies got here, Joe's sign was dead. But everyone was looking up and, well…" The Sheriff checked his watch and pointed to the Creedmore Building. "Give it a few seconds. It's on some kind of cycle."

Someone in the crowd started a countdown. "Ten, nine, eight, seven.…" Shep looked up at the night sky, to the dark form of the sign looming in the rain. "Six, five, four," the people continued as Shep shielded his eyes from the rain. A hum filled the air with the crowd's "three, two…."

And on perfect cue, a pop shattered the night and a shower of sparks flew across the face of the relit sign, bathing the upturned faces in a golden light. Joe's sign remained lit for only a few seconds before it blinked out once again, to the cheers of the crowd.

Shep turned to the Sheriff. "What the hell, Sheriff?"

Sheriff Tolar shrugged. "Joe and his helper are up on the roof, seeing what's going on. Looks like someone took a shot at the sign from the water tower."

"Any idea who?" Shep asked, though he knew he wouldn't like the answer.

"Well, no one saw the shooter, but one of my deputies said they passed Harlan's Silverado heading out to the ranch," Tolar said. "I sent Ted Bartley out to fetch him."

Before Shep could reply, the people started a second countdown. En masse, they cheered when the blaze of sparks shot forth across the sign and the lights raged. With a sigh, Shep turned to the Sheriff. "Boy, when he screws up, he does it big, don't he?"

The crowd began a third countdown. But this time, no shower of sparks accompanied their arrival at zero. There was no shower of sparks and the sign remained dark. Where there had been cheers, now there was a collective sigh. Vítor Barros emerged from the Creedmore Building with his son in tow. Vítor's hands were full of electrical equipment and a nest of bare wires. He offered the mayor and the sheriff a better view.

"Whoever fired upon the sign hit the main panel," Vítor said. He stuck a finger through the hole in a switch dangling loose at the end of a wire. "It was a very lucky shot to have hit this breaker in such a manner. The hole allowed in the rain to short out the connection. That was what caused the sparks."

Shep looked at the sheriff. "Well, what do we do about this?"

"Nobody saw who did it—"

"You and I both know who did it, Sheriff. Now what do we do?"

Sheriff Tolar turned to Joe. "How much do you think the damage is going to be?"

Joe shook his head. "Ain't that much, really. Couple of hundred for a new box?" He turned to Vítor, who agreed.

A car pulled up to the curb and Ted Bartley stepped out. He held the door open for Harlan, who stumbled into the street. "Found him out at the Ranch, drunk as a skunk and passed out in his truck."

Shep grabbed Harlan by the collar. "Son, what the hell were you thinking?"

Harlan just grunted in reply. Shep handed him off to the sheriff and turned back to Vítor. "I'm sorry. You were saying?"

"The sign can be fixed. It will take several weeks for new parts to arrive," Vítor said. He looked at the fist full of wires, then to the sign, as if reconsidering his solution. "But yes, it can be fixed."

Ted reached for the wires in Vítor's hand. "Weeks? There's no way we could do it quicker?"

Vítor shook his head. "I wish I could tell you more." He took the bundle of wires from Ted and turned back to the Creedmore Building. "I will lock the doors, Mr. Joe."

Shep glanced up at the sign and, as he turned for his car, his eyes caught the people on the square. Walking back to his car, he watched as the various conclaves broke up and headed back to their tents, their cars, anywhere to get out of the rain.

Chapter Thirty–Three

Harlan wasn't sure which was the worse pain: the hangover headache or the knotted muscle in the right side of his neck. He squinted against the glare of the fluorescent light above the bathroom sink and tried to force his eyes to focus. He had fallen asleep in the Lazy Boy sometime during the night, but moved to the guest bedroom around three, when he collapsed atop the comforter. In the harsh light of the bathroom mirror, the lines crisscrossing his face looked more like crimson rivers than pillow marks. He splashed cold water on his face and brushed his teeth. A hot shower would provide at least some relief to his neck.

Adjusting the water temperature, he smelled coffee from the kitchen. He showered, lingering longer than usual beneath the stream, and was drying off before he realized he heard none of the usual sounds coming from the kitchen. By this time on a Wednesday morning, Noreen should have been in full force to prepare her contributions to the church's food outreach for shut-ins. Most Wednesdays, even if Harlan wanted to sleep in, the noises and smells were so overwhelming that sleep was impossible. This morning, the house was silent.

He dressed quickly and headed for the kitchen. He found Noreen sitting at the kitchen table, a full cup of coffee on the saucer beside a plate of buttered toast. Harlan moved to kiss her on the cheek, but stopped when he saw what she was holding. In her hands was the reason the kitchen was silent and her coffee and toast untouched, the reason she was fighting to hold back the single tear welling in the corner of her eye. As soon as he saw the rain-damp, crumpled piece of paper, he recognized the V.A. letterhead and the thin, angular font of a medical statement.

He moved away quickly, poured himself a cup of coffee and considered his options. In his younger days, Harlan might have tried to play off such a discovery in anger. The bills were too detailed to lie. So he just sat beside her, in silence, and waited.

His own cup had gone cold and untouched by the time she spoke.

"I found it this morning, with the newspaper," she said, flatly. "It was there, on the porch. On the mat. I guess the paper boy saw it in the driveway and thought it looked important enough to put up with the paper."

She offered him the document, which he accepted. "Noreen, I–"

"Just don't," she interrupted. "I knew something was up. All those trips to Waco. The calls on your cell phone."

She chuckled halfheartedly.

He glanced up "What could possibly be funny about this?"

"Any other wife would have figured it was another woman. Given the choice between this and another woman, I'm not sure which one I'd pick."

He started to say something, but she held up her hand. "No. Don't. Not yet."

She stood, took her plate and both cups to the counter. While she moved about the kitchen, clanging pots and pans, Harlan saw a hummingbird hovering at the feeder and it triggered a memory of the day he and Carly were sitting on the back porch. It was an early morning not long after she'd come to live with them. She couldn't have been more than five or six. They were on the glider-swing, under the big picture window looking out over the back pasture. The sun was hanging low over the trees and it was going to be a hot day. But there was still a fresh hint of mist floating down across the alfalfa. He didn't remember what they were talking about, if anything. It was just one of a thousand such mornings, this one punctuated by the sickening crack and then thud of a hummingbird zooming into the window and falling onto the cushion between them.

When the bird first hit the window, Harlan was convinced it was dead. He looked down and saw it unmoving, the bird's green and blue neck twisted to the side. Before he could say anything, Carly scooped up the bird and held it. "Honey, I think it's dead," he said. She shook her head.

"Here." She formed his hand into a scoop and gently placed the bird in it. It weighed nothing and was motionless. But he could feel the heartbeat against his hand. Harlan extended his palm out to his niece. She stroked its neck, smoothed the ruffled feathers between its eyes. For almost ten minutes, the tiny delicate creature remained settled in his hand under the constant care of a child, until at last the bird's wings stirred. He extended his hand and it flew away.

Sitting in his kitchen now, Harlan thought for a moment he again felt the heartbeat of that hummingbird, frantic and strong. When Noreen placed the freshly warmed cup of coffee on the table before him, he realized it was his own pulse he felt.

"No more lies. No more hiding, and we'll talk about your secret post office box later," she said. She sat down again, but this time across the table from him. "Right now, all I want to know is if you're going to be okay."

He nodded, but then shrugged. "They want me to have surgery."

"It's that serious? You need surgery and you weren't going to tell–"

"No, baby. It wasn't that," he said. It was the first time in a long time he could remember calling her anything but Noreen.

"I was having this treatment, see. They put radiation in. But it's quit working."

"So you were getting radiation and not telling me?"

On this, he could not argue. "Yeah. But it was supposed to keep it in check. In almost everyone, it works but–"

"Your body's as stubborn as you?"

He chuckled. "Now they're saying surgery. But I'm not sure I want the surgery."

"What happens without it?"

When he didn't say anything, she just shook her head. "That's what I thought. When can we get you scheduled for the operation?"

"Noreen, I can't have it. I just can't. The doctor said it might...," but he trailed off, unwilling to finish his sentence.

"Might what, Harlan?"

He stood to leave the kitchen. She reached for his hand. "No, you stay. We're finishing this here. You're afraid of what? You won't be a man anymore?"

He just looked at her through clouding eyes.

She laughed. "Harlan, you think you'd be any less of a man if that happened? When was the last time–"

"Don't you finish that," he said. She winked at him.

"You done forgotten the most important part of all this, haven't you?"

"What's that?"

"You're Harlan Cotton. This ain't going to beat you. So get it together. Shep's called about half a dozen times this morning looking for you," she said. She kissed him on the cheek. "Said you need to come in and talk to the sheriff about last night. So you get on into town–and close that post office box while you're up there."

Chapter Thirty–Four

Rolling silverware had always been mind-numbing work for Doris, so boring she reduced the practice to a mantra. Napkin, knife, fork, spoon. Tuck, fold, roll. Deposit bundle. Repeat.

She placed a knife atop the napkin, fork atop the knife, with the bowl of the spoon resting firmly in the tines of the fork. After tucking the bottom, she would fold over the left side and roll to the right four times. Over the years, whenever Doris found the old milk crate where they kept rolled sets running low, she'd take the tub of clean utensils, slip into a booth near the door, and roll silverware, repeating her mantra again and again until, at last, the tub of utensils was empty and the crate filled with row upon row of perfect, white rolls.

Napkin, knife, fork, spoon. Tuck, fold, roll. Deposit bundle. Repeat.

She had been repeating for the better part of the last half-hour, this time out of necessity rather than boredom. She had discovered the crate was empty when she went to retrieve a bundle of silverware for a customer, a trucker who regularly stopped on the long haul between El Paso and St. Louis. As soon as she noticed the empty bin, she realized how long it had been since she had actually rolled silverware. She hadn't needed to for several days.

Business had pretty much evaporated.

Only four days had passed since Harlan killed Joe's sign, but in that time, a void washed through Cranston and filled every corner of the community with emptiness. The trucker, sitting at Joe's old booth and reading the newspaper, was only her third table of the morning. Even regulars weren't showing up.

Aside from the trucker, Greg Johnson and the Bartleys were the only customers the Café had seen so far. She checked the corner booth, where Ted and Margie were sandwiched in, hunched over and whispering almost conspiratorially across the table. They had been there all morning, occasionally joined by this person or that. For a while, old man Golson had joined them, though he only had one cup of coffee rather than his usual two. Even Jerry Franklin had wandered through, but he didn't stay for breakfast. Doris knew the reason for their shortened visits. They were in mourning.

"Ma'am?" came a call from the other end of the bar, where the visiting trucker was waiting patiently at the register. Doris placed the final bundle of silverware into the crate and smoothed her apron.

"How was your breakfast?" she asked, making the typical small talk banter she went through with all the out-of-towners.

The trucker didn't answer. Instead, his eyes trailed around the restaurant. "Where is everyone? Last time I was here, the place was hopping."

"Just a slow day, I guess," she said. But she knew that he knew she was lying. It wasn't just a slow day. "That'll be eight seventy-five."

He handed her a ten and a five. "Keep the change."

"Thanks," she said. "Catch you on the flip flop?"

He shrugged. "Route's changing next month. I don't know if I'll be back through. Things are changing too quickly."

He tipped his hat and was gone before Doris could reply. She watched as he crossed the lot to his truck. A group of boys were kicking a soccer ball around the parking lot near his rig. They cleared out quickly when he climbed into the cab.

By the time the trucker pulled onto the highway, Ted and Margie had made their way to the register and were waiting to pay. Doris went through the motions of ringing up their check in silence. "That'll be fifteen, even," she said.

Ted handed her a twenty. "Don't worry, Doris. Things are gonna pick up."

"I don't see how, but okay," Doris replied. She handed him five ones as change. He dropped two on the counter.

"Keep your chin up," he said. "We've got plans to get 'em back to town."

"What on earth are you talking about this time?" she said. He just smiled.

"I'm not supposed to say anything yet. But can you keep a secret?" Greg asked. He paused, waited for her to agree before continuing. "Well, remember how, after the big fireworks display, Joe raised the sign?"

She nodded again, a quiet fear spreading up the back of her neck.

"We're going to repeat it—every day," Margie said. "It'll be fabulous. All the businesses are for it. Shep's off talking to the Sheriff about additional security now. Isn't it exciting?"

Doris stood stunned, fuming for several seconds before she finally snapped. "Have you people lost your minds? That's the stupidest thing I've ever heard of, raising the sign over and over again. What? You want the fireworks too, I guess? Music? How about a rock band?"

When they didn't respond, Doris pressed on, a flood of anger washing over her. "Shep's in on it. I guess Harlan's ass deep in it too, huh? What the hell! Go for it. Let's just wreck everything, why don't we? What did Joe have to say when you told him? How did you convince him to go along with it?"

Ted and Margie exchanged guilty glances with Greg, glances Doris immediately understood.

"That's right. Nobody thought to ask Joe Morton, did they? Good ol' Joe. Gave his son so we all could be rich," she said. She began to tug frantically at her apron strings. The more she pulled, the tighter and more stubborn they got.

"Yep. Good old Joe Morton, right patriot that one is. Son's done died and–"

Doris yanked at her apron strings until one side broke loose and it came free in a crumple of fabric. She hurled it onto the bar with enough force to send an unfortunate salt shaker flying. Shep entered just in time to have to step out of the way of a salt shaker that her tossed apron sent flying. He watched, stunned, as it shattered on the floor at his feet.

"Doris, is there–" he began. She cut him off.

"You know what, Mayor? I've half a mind to drive out to Joe's place and tell him–"

He waved his hands frantically to stop her. "Doris, you won't find him."

Sheriff Tolar had come in behind him and nodded his agreement. "Joe's gone Bunny Carmichael on us."

"What do you mean?" she demanded.

"He's not there," Shep said. "We just came from Macomb Road. Mr. Barros said he's left town and has no plans to return."

Doris turned from Shep to the sheriff and then to Ted in disbelief. "He's...gone? Gone gone?"

Sheriff Tolar hung his head. Shep just shrugged.

"I don't believe...," she began, but her voice trailed off. The fact was, she could believe it. She couldn't blame Joe, even if his departure was sudden. She looked back to the sheriff again, still speechless.

Ted stood up from his spot and tried to rest a hand on her shoulder. When she brushed him away, he turned to the mayor and the sheriff. He was about to speak when Shep held up a hand to stop him.

"I don't know, Ted," the mayor said. "I don't know anything 'cept it looks like Joe's up and gone for good."

October: Doris Greely

Chapter Thirty–Five

Afternoons at the Truck Stop Café were easy, too easy in the months since Joe left. So Doris didn't mind when Jimmy called her into the kitchen one August morning to let her know he'd fired that useless girl from Grapeland and would need Doris to pull doubles "for a few days" until he found a replacement. Two days into the extra assignments, she told him not to bother. Even if most afternoons she was serving an empty dining room, it provided her with enough excuse to avoid going back home to the confines of those four rooms.

Doris appreciated the long afternoons of side work and filling coffee cups. Plus, the extra money could go towards the ten thousand dollars' worth of repairs Vítor Barros said it would take if she wanted to safely reoccupy the second floor of her house. Between the extra shifts and the money Vítor paid her to continue Téo's tutoring, she figured she would be able to move back into at least her bedroom by spring. Plus, the longer hours at the Café were a relaxing change of pace from the breakfast crowd. About the time the sun started to hit the horizon in the evenings, a little rush of regulars popped in for burgers and chicken plates on their way home. By October, she was so used to the extra-long days she barely noticed until one evening she realized she had left her house before sun up and would be returning after dark.

She was bussing a table of three that had just left when Jimmy rang the bell in the window. Almost by instinct, she started for the window, but stopped when she realized the Café was empty.

"Whatcha need, Jimmy?" she called over her shoulder. She lifted the bus tub and slid it onto the counter.

"It's dead. I have a to-go coming in about six thirty," he said. "Noreen's picking up a plate for Harlan. You can go ahead and go, if you'd like."

"Nah. I'll wait on Noreen. I want to know how Harlan's doing," she said. "You haven't heard have you?"

"Not since before the surgery," Jimmy said. "So we shut down when she gets here?"

She pondered the question for a moment, but couldn't muster a strong opinion either way. While her feet ached and a hot bath would be nice, closing early meant she would have to go home. It was hard to get excited about trading one prison cell for another.

Jimmy nodded his final decision. "That's what we'll do. Look at the bright side. Tomorrow's Sunday. We can both catch up on our beauty sleep."

"Hey! You trying to tell me something?"

"Yeah. Haven't you noticed these bags under my eyes?" he said.

She laughed. "Sleeping in will be nice."

She certainly understood his desire to shut the restaurant down early. After all, it cost money to keep the lights on. And there weren't a whole lot of people beating down the door for a late dinner these days. Despite their best attempts to restore the sign to its former prominence in the public eye, the Cranston Chamber of Commerce couldn't do anything to attract the crowds that left the night of the shooting. Three months after the sign first appeared, life seemed to have returned to normal.

After wiping down the booth, Doris tossed the wet rag onto the counter with a plop and hoisted the bus tub onto her hip.

"I'll load these into the washer for you if you'll keep an eye on the front," she said as she backed through the butler's door to the kitchen. Jimmy was leaning against the refrigerator, an unlit cigarette dangling from his lips.

She shot him a sideways look. "You shouldn't be smoking in the kitchen."

"Yeah, because I might ash in all these customers' food," he said as he stooped down and touched the tip of the cigarette to a lit burner on the empty stove.

The dishwasher was a stainless steel box that lived under a lean-to on the back wall of the Café. It took her only a minute or so to load the entire bus tub into the heavy plastic tray that slid into the washer and she slammed the door down with the handle that always reminded her of the handle on a slot machine. The machine roared to life and Doris rested against the doorframe and smoked a cigarette of her own. The air was bordering on crisp and she made a mental note to spend part of Sunday moving her fall and winter clothes from the cedar closet to the coat closet that was now home to her main wardrobe. She snuffed the butt against the cinderblock wall and opened the washer to retrieve the now clean rack of dishes.

She stepped in and poked her head into the kitchen. "You want me to put these–" she began. She stopped when she realized Jimmy wasn't there.

Doris found him leaning on the counter, talking to someone seated on the other side.

"Well, this late I guess I'd recommend the hamburger," he was saying. "Though I could fry you up some chicken if you'd like."

Doris stepped up to the counter and flopped her ticket book down beside Jimmy. "You want to write it up for me and I cook it?"

He chuckled. "Nah, you take it. Mr. Groot, she'll take care of you from here. Order whatever you'd like."

"I do not wish to inconvenience you, though," the stranger said. "A hamburger will be good. Yes."

"Comin' right up," Jimmy said.

"What can I get you to drink?" Doris asked.

"A Coca-Cola?" he replied. He lifted the end of the sentence, almost as if asking a question rather than placing an order. She also thought she detected the hint of an accent.

"You ain't from around here, are you?"

He nodded. "I am from Holland."

"Figured as much." She sat the soda glass on the counter harder than usual. That was when she noticed his vest. It was one of the khaki numbers she had grown an aversion to during the media invasion, when it seemed every other man in the restaurant was wearing one. "You won't be here long, will you?"

"I ordered a hamburger," he said.

"No. I mean you're here for the sign. You won't be very long, right?"

A blank stare told her that he did not understand.

"The sign? The big F You?"

He shook his head. "I do not know of this sign."

"If you ain't here for the sign, then why are you here?"

"I came to make a funeral," he said.

Doris immediately recognized her mistake and her cheeks went flush. "I am so sorry. I saw the vest and just assumed you're another reporter."

"Ah. The vest! Yes. I am a documentary filmmaker. I film nature."

"Like animals and stuff?"

"Yes. Animals, mostly. But also trees and other things."

She was about to ask him what sorts of things when Jimmy rang the bell. When she turned to pick up the plate, he shot her a look. "Don't be pissing off the only customer."

"So I made a mistake. Shoot me."

Doris delivered the burger and left the man to eat in peace. A few minutes later, he called her. "Miss."

"You can call me Doris," she said. Doris saw that he needed a refill and brought him a fresh glass. He thanked her and took a long draw from the glass.

"I am Karl Groot. It is nice to meet you. Doris."

Chapter Thirty–Six

When Doris's phone rang early Sunday morning, she figured it was Margie calling to gossip about church business. She was pleasantly surprised to see Jimmy's number flashing on the caller I.D. instead. She pressed the talk button. Before the phone was to her ear, Jimmy was talking.

"Harlan's coming to breakfast tomorrow morning and Ted's got the whole damned town coming out. Think you can come in a few minutes early? I'll give you the afternoon off," he said.

She reached for her alarm clock and dialed back the alarm to four-thirty. "See you at five?"

"You're a doll. And don't ever let anybody tell you different," he said. "We'll close up early tomorrow so you can have the afternoon off."

The line went dead before she could reply, plunging her back into the merciless silence of her empty house. She looked around at what had once been a comfortable and cozy living room and sighed. Houses told stories. At that moment, Doris did not like the story her house was telling.

The television was mostly blocked by the corner of her dresser. Along the wall that once held only a small bureau and two occasional chairs, the sofa now competed for space with a nightstand and the dirty laundry basket. Vítor had been nice enough to disassemble the dining room table and stand it behind the sofa to free up that space for a makeshift bedroom. She had even lost the kitchen to her mirrored vanity. The confined quarters, though, were not the worst part for Doris. Making her way to the bathroom, she passed the mottled comforter tacked over the archway at the foot of the stairs. The blanket was a feeble attempt to save a little money on the utility bill by trapping the cold air downstairs. But the comforter wafted in the draft, which lent a sense of the space beyond, a space that every day grew more and more confining. Sitting in the winged back lounger in the living room, Doris tried to ignore the blanket by turning on the television with hopes of finding a distracted hour or two there.

The next morning, Doris reported to the Café at five a.m. and found Jimmy hard at work on breakfast preparations. Margie was already there and had covered all the tables with plastic table cloths. At the center of each table, the normal setup of salt and pepper shaker, ketchup and mustard was gone. In its place, she set what looked to Doris like a demented party hat with tinsel exploding out of it. Across the ceiling over the bar there hung a banner, which in a loud and cheerful font shouted, "Welcome Back Harlan!" Beneath the banner, Jimmy was adjusting the flames under a carefully aligned row of chafing dishes.

"Buffet style, today?"

"Ted's idea," he said. "We'll skip the menu this morning. Eight bucks for the buffet."

By seven-thirty, it was apparent Ted's suggestion proved to be a good one. Every seat in the house was full, except for Harlan's normal spot in the corner, which was guarded by a hovering bouquet of balloons taped to the seat of the booth. Just in case the balloons were not enough of a hint to keep Harlan's seat empty, Margie was keeping one eye trained on the corner. At least twice, she shooed one of the Johnson boys out of the seat. The place was so crowded that Doris was having trouble carrying a coffee pot through the restaurant without sloshing half of it onto the floor every time she brushed past someone. Finally, she fled behind the bar. If they wanted coffee, they could come to her for a change.

Through the window, Doris watched the sidewalk, where an overflow crowd had begun to take shape. Someone brought down a load of folding tables and chairs. Ted was marshaling the unload. With the help of Shep and a couple of church deacons, he turned half a dozen parking places into a makeshift dining area. Without asking, Margie began removing the chafing dishes to a table outside. On her second trip in, the impropriety of making such a change without first asking permission struck Margie.

"Honey, you don't mind if we take a few of these outside, do you?" she asked. Without waiting for an answer, she continued. "It'll just make it so much easier for Harlan to get to his seat when he gets here."

Doris forced a smile. "That's fine, Margie. In fact, will you keep an eye on the front? I'm in desperate need of coffee cups and they're out back, in the washer."

"Oh! Go! Yes, go. We can't run out of cups right now. The whole town's come out."

Doris untied her apron and slipped it under the bar on top of the full rack of clean cups. "Thanks, Margie. I'll try to be quick," she said.

Out back, Doris pulled up a stack of empty plastic milk crates over beside the dishwasher and sat down. A breeze was whipping up dust devils in the empty parking lot behind the Café. It carried with it the occasional tinkle of laughter and voices. She lit a cigarette and took a long drag deep into her lungs. The back door opened and Jimmy appeared, an unlit cigarette dangling from his lips.

"There you are," he said.

She moved to stand. "They need something?"

He motioned her to sit back down. "They're fine. Let 'em fend for themselves for a bit. Besides," he said, lighting the cigarette. "We're out."

"Out of?"

"Yes," he said, exhaling a long jet of smoke. "Eggs. Bread. Biscuits. Hash browns. You name it, it's gone."

"Want me to run to the store?"

He shook his head. "No, stay put. We run out, we're out. I'm already losing money on this deal," he said. "It'll just make it worse with the wife if I go spending the cash in the register."

This was the first time Jimmy had ever mentioned business to Doris. She never wondered whether that was because matters of finance were none of her business or because Jimmy just assumed she knew because she worked the register. Under the back awning now, Doris could see the concern in Jimmy's face.

"How bad is it?"

He looked away without responding.

"Business has been steady, or at least as steady as it was before everything," she said. "So what's going on?"

"Customers are steady. Business, not so much. They're buying less, or just drinking coffee." He lit another cigarette and offered Doris one, which she declined.

"Everybody went crazy with spending for the few weeks after the Fourth, and now they're all broke."

Doris was about to speak when they both noticed a swell in the noise out front. Someone popped a head into the dining room and shouted, "Here he comes!"

Jimmy tossed the lit cigarette into the sand-filled coffee can and motioned Doris to follow. Back in the dining room and out on the makeshift patio, everyone was watching as Noreen's Lincoln rolled into the parking lot. She waved enthusiastically as it came to a stop in the handicapped space. A hush crept across the crowd as Noreen and Harlan exchanged words, their lips moving silently behind the windshield. At last, Noreen turned off the car and got out. She waved again and smiled before rushing around to the passenger side and opening Harlan's door. He brushed aside her extended hand and instead braced himself against the door and pulled himself out and up. He steadied himself against the roof of the car. It was clear that the surgery and chemo had taken their toll on him. But with a determination Doris found admirable, he took his first step toward the sidewalk and everyone burst into cheers.

He stopped in his tracks and just stared at them from beneath the brim of a tan Stetson. One by one everyone fell silent. When at last silence prevailed, Harlan cleared his throat and looked directly at Ted and Margie Bartley.

"You shouldn't have," he said.

"It was nothing, Harlan. Proud to–" Ted said, but Harlan hushed him.

"No. You really shouldn't have," Harlan said.

He climbed back into the car, slammed the door, and pulled his hat down over his face. Noreen's shoulders slumped and she tried to smile as she made her way back to the driver's side. As the Lincoln disappeared out of sight around the bend, Ted sighed and turned to the sheriff.

"I guess we'll just pack up and call it a day."

Chapter Thirty–Seven

Clearing away the remains of Harlan's welcome home party took the better part of the morning. As Doris hoisted the last bag of paper plates into the dumpster, she was relieved to have it behind her. Ted's intentions may have been admirable, but inviting the whole town without so much as asking Harlan if he was ready for such a show of force was shortsighted. Despite wanting to run things, Harlan was a private man suffering through a private crisis. He probably didn't appreciate Ted bringing the whole town into it. She slammed the lid of the dumpster and wiped her hands on her apron.

She heard a noise from under the awning and saw Jimmy at the washer, loading the last of the chafing dishes into a rack. Doris tried to judge his frustration level by measuring the volume with which the trays made contact in the rack. The ferocity of each movement grew such that, by the time she was back up to the building, he slammed the door of the washer with such anger the machine failed to start, forcing him to open and close the door again. She ducked into the building without stopping, denying him the chance to vent any of his growing anger on her. She'd seen Jimmy in a bad mood once, fifteen years before, and had no desire to repeat the experience.

Back in the dining room, she found a pleasant face waiting patiently. Karl was sitting at the bar, reading a book.

"Welcome back, Karl!" she said.

"Thank you. Is it too late for breakfast?"

"Normally, I'd say no. But this morning I'd recommend a cheeseburger and fries."

He handed her the menu by way of agreement. "If you would, I will let you know when I am ready? I am meeting a Mr. Gruber here concerning a personal matter."

Doris almost asked, but the way he had said personal matter was enough of a flag that she didn't press. Instead, she smiled. "That'll be fine, Karl. Would you like some coffee or a glass of iced tea?"

"Hot tea, if you have it," he said.

It took her a moment to find the small basket of tea bags Cash left behind and she spread them out on the counter to take stock. "I can offer you Earl Grey, chamomile or Darjeeling."

He looked up from his book and considered his options. "Let's start with the chamomile. But I may change to the Darjeeling later. Yes?"

Doris held up the single chamomile bag. "If you want more than one cup, that'll be exactly what happens."

She went to the coffee pot and used the hot water spout to heat the mug as Cash had shown her. When the cool earthenware became warm to the touch, Doris emptied it into the sink and refilled it, quickly dropping in the teabag before covering the mug with a saucer. She placed the saucer-mug combination gently to the right of Karl's book.

"So what are you reading?"

He held up the book to reveal to her the brightly colored cover of a spy novel by an author she'd never heard of. "It is a beach book I picked up in the airport. Do you like to read?"

"Yes," she answered. What was she saying? She rarely read anything but silly tabloids. "I just don't ever have the time anymore."

Her book preferences were apparently more interesting to her customer than his own book, which he had closed and returned to the counter. "I love to read. When I travel for work I take with me so many books I think I should put them in their own suitcase! Who is your favorite author?"

She froze. The names of all the authors of the day suddenly escaped her. Doris was about to answer, to lie, when he saved her.

"I love so many writers. The works of your Lost Generation are good, no?"

Lost generation. Lost generation. That was something from high school.

"And I especially like the works of the Latin Americans today. Brazil has produced so many great writers, don't you think?"

Unwittingly, he had delivered to her the opening to change the subject. She nodded her agreement. "In fact, Karl, we have a man from Brazil who lives here in Cranston. He usually comes in with his son for a late lunch. If you are still here, I'll introduce you."

"He likes books, yes?"

"He is very intelligent," Doris said. She excused herself and fled to the kitchen, unsure why she had just fabricated a literary interest with a complete stranger. Maybe he had assumed she would not like books. That would explain his excitement. Just because she was from Podunk, East Texas, didn't mean she didn't know books. Her cheeks were flushed and, without a thought, she plunged into the cool iciness of the walk-in freezer. The stacked cases of French fries provided a cold, solid leaning surface. Doris watched the ice crystals dance in the air each time she exhaled. After a few seconds, she chuckled. Karl was just a man. A man who wasn't even from here. He would be leaving in a few days and that would be that. Of course, leaving the walk-in empty handed after a couple of minutes of absence would look strange, so she grabbed a stick of butter before returning to the dining room.

At least Karl was again engrossed in his book. She deposited the butter in the small refrigerator under the counter. With the hollow thud of an empty mug against the Formica, Doris's time expired. She would have to talk to him again.

"Ready for another cup?"

"Hmm?" He looked up from his book. "No, I think I will be okay for now. You will let me know when Mr. Gruber arrives, yes? Do you know Mr. Gruber?"

"Small town," she said.

"Ah, yes. I live in a small town as well." He smiled at her. "It is not too much different from your Cranston. Near to the sea. And it is much colder! My wife asks always if we cannot move to the south of France."

"So you're married?"

He reached for his wallet and removed a small, plastic sheath photo. She took it. His wife was kneeling between two boys with impossibly blonde hair. "That's some pair of cotton tops you got."

"Cotton tops?"

She pointed to the boys' hair. "Yeah. That's almost white!"

When he laughed, it was the too loud, boisterous laugh of familiarity and again, Doris found herself leaning on the counter and laughing with him. He told her about traveling the world, about filming the snows on Kilimanjaro for a documentary, about the lion that took his partner's camera while they slept in their tent. Here was a man who had seen the world, done things, but could just as soon have been her next door neighbor.

"How have you never been to Europe, Doris?"

"Karl, I've never been to Louisiana," she said. When he did not register Louisiana, she sighed. "It's the next state over."

"You should come sometime! We would show you a really good time."

"That'll never happen," she said. "Someone's got to stay and keep Jimmy in line. Ain't that right Jimmy?"

Jimmy dropped the rack of clean glasses onto the counter. "You can go to Europe if you want, doll. Just put those up and refill the salt shakers first."

She popped the bar towel at him, but any reply would have to wait. The bells chimed against the glass. Frederick Gruber had arrived. He saw the trio at the bar and approached, his hand extended to Karl.

"Mr. Groot?"

Karl stiffened as he stood and shook Frederick's hand. "I thank you for meeting me somewhere I knew."

Frederick's smile was warm and pleasant. "Mr. Groot, please. It is my job to make you as comfortable as possible during times such as these. Would you care to sit with me for a moment? Perhaps lunch?"

"Doris suggested a hamburger."

Frederick agreed. "Make it two cheeseburgers, with fries."

She watched Frederick usher her Karl away from the counter. It was the same compassion he had shown Joe at Casey's memorial service. But their discussion was none of her concern and she instead busied herself with refilling the salt shakers and straightening up behind the bar. Though she desperately tried to prevent herself from focusing on their conversation, Doris could not help but wonder about this man and his connection to Cranston. That a European documentary filmmaker would have need of a funeral home's services in her little town strained reason. Yet, there he sat at table five, munching on french fries and reviewing the various papers Frederick passed to him. After one final review, Karl signed a series of papers and handed them back to Frederick. He stopped at the door long enough to say good bye to her.

"I will see you for breakfast tomorrow. Yes?"

"Don't plan on being anywhere else," she replied. Before the door closed behind him, Doris was at table five. Ostensibly, she would bus the table. In reality, though, she had only one goal.

"What's up with Karl?"

Frederick looked up from his paperwork. "Mr. Groot? He is securing a resting place for his mother."

Something wasn't clicking. "Why would Karl bury his mama here? He's from–"

"Not Karl," Frederick said, emphasizing the L. "His name is Car. Like you drive. As in Carmichael. His mother was from here, but left probably before you were out of diapers."

The blood rushed from Doris's head and she had to sit down. All of Mama's stories about Bunny Carmichael had instilled in her a sense of reverence reserved for cautionary tales and mythical heroines. Depending on Mama's mood, Bunny could be "the one who made it out," or "the crazy woman who abandoned everyone and everything familiar just to." If Doris had to pick, she would have been hard pressed to decide which of the gods of her youth exerted more influence: Bunny Carmichael or God himself. And she had just spent the morning talking to Jesus Christ, or at least the Bunny Carmichael version of him.

Chapter Thirty-Eight

Doris awoke with a start and almost tumbled from the sofa. She steadied herself on the coffee table for a moment, to give herself time to catch her bearings. The sun was streaming through the front window, bathing the room in a soft yellow glow. As her mind emerged from the fog of a Flexeril-induced sleep, Doris thought for a split-second the sunlight was a sign of morning, that she had somehow slept through the night, and she bolted upright on the sofa. But as soon as her head recovered from the dizziness of rising too suddenly, she saw the clock on the mantle, ticking its way quietly toward five o'clock. In the corner, the muted television flickered travel program images of tourists strolling along the wide boulevard of some sun-drenched coastal city. Her stomach rumbled its objections to her afternoon nap.

Smacking her lips, Doris realized she was thirsty and needed to brush her teeth before heading out to find food. As she made her way to the bathroom, she tried to remember more of the dream that had jarred her awake, but it was all a jumble.

She was able to recall a storm blowing through Cranston. A hard, cold wind whipped through the streets, kicking up clouds of dust and debris from the makeshift campground on the square. There were people huddled in the storm, close to the buildings. No matter how hard she tried, Doris could not remember if she had seen their faces. Then, something had awakened her. A crash, maybe? A cataclysmic bang. Yes, that was it. Almost thunder, but artificial. Brushing her teeth, she closed her eyes and strained, reaching for the answer before the haze, the fog of the dream could vanish for good. Then she saw it.

Joe's sign.

The wind had ripped Joe's sign from the roof and hurled it into the square below. That's why the people had been huddled near to the buildings, covering their heads. The sign was crashing down upon them. But there was something else, some vague, nebulous part of the dream. Doris blotted her mouth dry and tried again to remember more of the details, as if somehow, unlocking the dream might give her the answer to a difficult riddle.

She wasn't stationary in the dream. The wind was carrying her along with the debris. The debris, the dust was all moving in one direction; the wind was blowing it all out of town and carrying her with it. The shape she had seen at the end of her dream was the town limits sign, receding quickly.

For the first time since entering the bathroom, Doris allowed her eyes to focus on her reflection in the mirror. There were lines around her eyes, which themselves were tired and sagging. Each corner of her mouth sported the deep ravines of two decades of the fake smiles of customer appreciation. Her hair had begun to gray at the temples and at her widow's peak. She could see faint remnants of a once graceful beauty, but years of East Texas summers had eroded that charm. Now, only the slightest smudges of blush on her cheeks kept her customers from noticing that which she herself was just realizing. Age hadn't been as kind to Doris as she had once believed. Here she stood in the tiniest bathroom of her increasingly tiny house with little to show for her tiny life.

She wasn't sure what she had expected, all those years ago, when she decided to forego marriage in favor of life as "a career woman." Independence? The world of adventure Bunny's story promised? If either was the case, then she was a complete failure. Aside from the last six months, what adventure had those thirty years brought her? Doris always knew the world was never going to come to Cranston, but she had at least hoped a part of it would find its way into her life. Joe's sign had made that happen for her, at least briefly.

She chuckled. At least she now knew what espresso was and how to make a cappuccino. That accounted for a pretty good start, she reckoned, and at least it wasn't lost. She could hear the voice of her mother, some ten years dead, chiding her for this momentary indulgence.

"Anytime you start feeling sorry for yourself, figure out why," her mother would say. "Then, think of someone who might be feeling bad about the same thing and go cheer them up. That'll teach you not to feel sorry for yourself."

It took her less than a second to decide what really had her down. She wasn't sad because she was old. She was alone and lonesome. Did that give her the right to feel sorry for herself? After all, just think about Joe for a minute. He had been lonely, too, she realized, and his was a situation much worse than hers. Joe's loneliness wasn't by his choice, after all, and it was just a bit more permanent. Somewhere in a motel room, Car Groot was dealing with burying his mother. Doris knew that kind of pain. Talk about lonesome. When she buried Mama, she was surrounded by friends. The whole town came out. That's something Car would not have.

And there, before the mirror, Doris realized Mama was right. She only had to find a person feeling especially lonely this afternoon.

She blotted her eyes to remove stray specks of mascara and fixed her hair back into place. She took one final second, smiled at her progress and hoped the pink glow of a deep sleep in her cheeks would fade before she made it to the motel across town. And if not, Carmichael Groot wouldn't care that she had taken a nap in the afternoon. She grabbed her purse from the coffee table, tossed her cell phone into the largest pocket and snatched her car keys from the hook by the door. Doris wasn't sure what she expected to say or do when she arrived. She wasn't even entirely sure the idea of just showing up at his doorstep wasn't some half crazy whim she would have been better off ignoring. All she knew as she slammed the car door and started the engine was the almost tactile sensation that, like Cranston, she had turned a corner and now there was no going back.

Chapter Thirty-Nine

Bunny Carmichael's ideas were always a little out of place in Cranston. Maybe that's why she had left at such a young age and didn't return until after she was dead. At least that's what the few people there told themselves as they huddled past the makeshift memorial Frederick Gruber had assembled on the table at the front of the smallest of the two memorial chapels at Gruber Family Funeral Home. The display consisted wholly of photographs provided by Car for the occasion. The photos were all scenes from her life.

Bunny picnicking at the Sphinx.

Bunny wading in Trevi Fountain.

Bunny and an infant Car dining in a Café on the Champs Elysées.

Bunny at sixty, in a helmet and harness, tethered to a zip line in the jungle.

It was the last that Doris had fixed upon when she first came to the table. It was one of only two color images and was the one that best highlighted the particular free spirit that took her out of Cranston in the first place. One of the other visitors brushed past her and she realized she was lingering too long in front of the photos and should probably move on to the second table. But she couldn't bring herself to do so. The second table was decorated only with a spray of tiger lilies and a large over-framed and matted glamour portrait on either side of an alabaster urn holding what was left of Bunny.

It was the first time in Doris's life anyone had displayed an urn at Gruber's. People didn't get cremated. They got buried in Memorial Park or, if they preferred, at the Old Baptist Cemetery. Cremation just wasn't natural and the thought of lying in a burning box gave Doris a shiver up her spine. Better to get it over quickly. She lingered a second longer. Car was meeting one of his new Carmichael cousins. If she lingered a moment, she could make eye contact and rush over, avoiding a stop at the second table. She stooped low to examine a photograph of a young Bunny and a toddler Car posing with a uniformed guard at Buckingham Palace. In the toddler's face, she could see the outlines of what would eventually grow into the man at the end of the receiving line. At last, his cousin gone, Doris smiled at him and passed the urn without even a pause.

"How you holding up, Car?"

He was confused. "I am fine. Why?"

Doris indicated the table. "It's your mama's funeral."

He chuckled. "Ah! No, I'm sorry. She passed away some time back. I've only just been able to come home–"

Doris blushed at her own ignorance. Of course Bunny wasn't recently dead. That's why people were cremated.

"I just assumed. I'm sorry," she said.

Car suddenly grew very serious and led her to a nearby chair. "I am very glad you came. I have a favor I would like to ask. Very serious."

She sat and he pulled a chair in front of her. He leaned in. "I made a list of places I would like to visit. Would you show me them? I would like very much to make a movie about my mother's home."

She laughed. "Car, that's... of course I'll show you. But there ain't that much to see. I'm afraid you'll be–"

"Thank you," he said. He almost leapt from his seat. "I will get my camera and–"

She reached out for his hand. "Now? I thought you meant–"

"Of course! I want to see the places my mother spoke of so often. The sawmill? There was a creek where she swam with your mother as children. And of course I want to–"

"Slow down, Car!" she said.

But Car didn't slow down. And he had indeed made a list, which he presented to Doris on a single leaf of paper in childlike block letters. Twenty minutes after leaving the funeral home, Car bounded from the car at the old saw mill and slung his camera bag over his shoulder. He called to her over his shoulder.

"Would you please bring the tripod, yes?"

She looked over the back seat of the rental car for his tripod. It was on the floorboard, sandwiched between his briefcase and an overstuffed duffle bag. The tripod was heavy and she had to tug to get it over the seat. By the time she caught up with Car, his camera was resting on his shoulder. She rested the tripod against her hip as he moved about around the superintendent's shack. The ancient mill, long abandoned, still held much of the mechanisms that once made the building hum with life. At one end, a windstorm had torn the roof back and the sheets of tin were coiled into a spiral that reminded her of old sardine cans. The weeds and grass got taller closer to the building, so tall that a couple of times, she lost sight of Car. The second time, he reappeared and relieved her of the tripod.

"I just need one more shot. This one, I'll use the tripod for," he said.

She watched with interest as he mounted the camera onto the tripod and locked the latch on the side. Each movement had purpose and a skill behind it so that there was little wasted energy. A twist of his wrist and the camera moved in one direction. Another twist, it pivoted back again. Doris was impressed with the smoothness of each action. There was a word, but she couldn't place it on her tongue. These were skills he was no doubt trained for, and to watch the care he took in filming an old shed and some broken equipment made her wonder what kind of effort filming his wildlife videos took.

Car flipped the camera off and unhooked it from the tripod. "What is next? The creek?"

"Whatever you want," she said. "It'll take a walk to get to, though."

They drove out to the county fairground and parked beneath the shade of one of the pear trees the county had planted. Her arm extended, she traced the line of the horizon. "All of this used to belong to your family," she said. "Well, the Cranston Charmichaels."

"Really? This is a lot of land!"

Doris squinted at the horizon. "Hm. It's about five hundred acres in this tract. Then the Cotton place and Ted and Margie Bartley's. You know them from–"

"From the hotel. Yes."

"Then, Joe's place and the other part of the Carmichael lands. That's the part your people still own. It's about five miles that way." She pointed toward the sun and started walking.

"We aren't going to walk all that way, are we?"

She laughed. "No. The creek's at the back of the fairgrounds. Mama and Bunny used to sneak down here on the weekends with some of the area boys. To swim."

He nodded appreciatively. "Yes, to swim."

She smacked him on the shoulder. "No, silly. They were good girls back then. They didn't do that sort of thing. In fact, I doubt my mama ever went skinny dipping."

Car looked away sheepishly.

"What?" she said.

"She skinny dipped. And drank moonshine liquor. Ma always said your ma was the wild one of the bunch."

Doris giggled. Of course he'd say that. His mother was the one that ran off to see the world.

"It is true. Ma said all your ma ever talked about was running away. Always 'got her goat' that my ma was the one who did it," he said. He stopped. "Doris, what is this 'got her goat'?"

"It means–" she began, but she had to stop. "Some things can't be translated, I guess."

This answer seemed to satisfy him, for he nodded and struck off again. A nice breeze tickled the short grass of the grounds. October evenings in Texas could be as brutal as a summer day. Doris was thankful today decided to be nicer to them. The creek lay at the bottom of a small, rocky valley that cut through the middle of the old Carmichael homestead. The descent was, from the direction of road, a comfortable walk. She knew they were close when the bleached bones of the sycamore tree came into view. Car stopped a few paces later.

"I wish I had brought my microphone," he said. "Can you hear that?"

She strained to listen, but all she could hear was the wind and the babble of the creek a couple dozen yards away. "Hear what?"

"The water. Just like Ma told me," he said. "We must be very close.

He snatched the tripod from her and rushed ahead through the grass. Doris picked up her pace to follow him. Somewhere between the first sight of the sycamore and the banks of the creek, she came to understand his sense of excitement and awe. Just as she had grown up hearing stories of Bunny Carmichael's fabulous, mystifying life abroad, Car Groot grew up with tales about life in Cranston. Car knew the Eiffel Tower and the palaces of Europe. He traveled through deserts and jungles to places Doris could barely imagine. It was places like the rocky creek running under this sycamore tree that had filled Car's imagination for his whole life. And for this brief moment, as he waded ankle deep into the water, Doris began to share his sense of awe at a creek she'd seen a hundred times.

Chapter Forty

"You going to breakfast this morning or you just gonna keep hiding?" Noreen asked. Harlan just grunted and stared at the front page of the Sun-Times. Noreen didn't seem deterred and pressed on.

"Doctor called back this morning and said it's okay for you to drive after three weeks."

Harlan's ears perked. He hadn't been behind the wheel since before the surgery. This was good news indeed and, for just a moment, he felt like he did the first morning his father allowed him to drive the old farm truck. He liked this feeling and let his mind linger on that emotion before grumbling under his breath.

"What, Harlan? You know I can't stand it when you mumble," Noreen said. He slapped the paper shut.

"I said fine, if you're that damned pressed to get me out of the house," he said. "So long as Ted don't alert Dan Rather."

She took the paper from him and opened it. "I don't think Ted would cross the road to see you after the way you acted. You should apologize when you see him."

"Me? For what?"

"For being a whole lot Harlan Cotton the other day," she said.

She was right. Harlan still didn't know quite why he had reacted with such anger. It was just seeing everyone out like that, at once, all excited and for what? He went and caught cancer then had to have surgery just to go on living. If this is what you call living, he thought as he adjusted the colostomy bag.

"Still smarting?" Noreen asked.

"A little," he said.

"Just remember, you're one of the lucky ones. It's only for a few months. Doc says you're a good candidate for reversal, once you heal up," she said. "Go get dressed. Your keys are on the hook."

He kissed her on the cheek and made for the bedroom. She was right. From everything the doctors told him in Waco, the colostomy was only a temporary inconvenience. For that, he was thankful. Removing his night shirt, Harlan passed in front of a mirror and stopped. He held his hand over the bag, to hide it. Were it not for the bag and the scar snaking around the side of his abdomen, he would have been pleased to look like he did. The surgery and chemotherapy meant weight loss and he could have stood to lose a few pounds anyway. Temporary colostomy or not, there were still other things that had yet to bounce back. Until that happened, which the surgeon assured him would happen in its own time, he would continue to feel like less of a man.

He dressed quickly and rushed from the house just in case Noreen changed her mind. He was halfway to the Café when he realized he did not have his cell phone or wallet. But he didn't turn around. Jimmy would just have to trust him for the cost of a cup of coffee and a biscuit or two. He turned into the parking lot later than he would have liked, but that was a blessing in itself. Ted's car was already gone and it looked like he would be able to enjoy his breakfast in relative peace. He pulled the Silverado into his usual spot by the edge of the lot, but stopped short of putting the car into park. With a moment's consideration, he let off the brake and coasted the truck in between the two blue lines. If he was going to be a half a man, however temporarily, he would at least enjoy one of the few perks.

He hung his hat and jacket on the coat rack by the door. Doris must have seen him from the parking lot, because sitting on his table was a cup of steaming coffee. He sat down, inhaled the aroma deeply, but stopped.

"You change coffees on me, Doris?"

She shook her head. "Nope. It's decaf. Noreen said I wasn't to serve you the full strength stuff unless I wanted you to come live with me and pay your medical bills. Doctor's orders."

She was walking away before he thought of any sort of response. So much for the freedom of a car.

"You want the paper?" Doris asked.

"Read it already," he replied. "Maybe the crossword. And a biscuit?"

The bells rang and he looked up to find a stranger in the doorway. The man saw Doris and smiled.

"Hello again. I have something for you to see, Doris," the man said. Whoever this man was, he was no stranger. Harlan pulled himself to his feet.

"Hey. Harlan Cotton," he said.

The man offered him a hand. "Car Groot."

Doris emerged from the kitchen with a plate of biscuits. "Harlan, don't you go scaring off my customers now."

Car set a laptop on the counter and opened it. "I worked on this all night. Just so I could show you what came of yesterday."

He inserted a disk into the drive and the machine purred. Harlan and Doris watched for a moment as the screen went blank. Then, the old saw mill drifted into view. A woman's voice came up over the video, soft, a bit shaky at first, but strong. The narrator was describing the scene.

"You see now," Car said. "I play this at Ma's memorial back home. Her friends will come to see it."

Harlan leaned in. "I recognize that voice, don't I?"

"Did you know my ma?" Car asked.

"Who was your ma?" Harlan asked, but he didn't wait for a reply. "That's Bunny, ain't it?"

Car nodded enthusiastically as he clicked to pause the video. "Yes! My ma! You knew her?"

"She babysat me until I was about ten. Put my mother over the edge when she left town," Harlan said. "So you're Bunny Carmichael's boy. If that don't beat all. Want to join me for breakfast?"

Harlan led him over to his booth and motioned to a seat. "So what brings you back to Cranston?"

He listened as Car told him about the past few days, about Bunny's memorial service, about the tour of the area.

"You should've let me know he was here, Doris. I'd have taken him out to the old home place," Harlan said. "Car, would you like to see where your ma was born?"

"May I bring my camera?"

"Of course. I'll have to call Ted and let him know we're crossing his place, but that won't be a problem. You're at the motel?"

Car nodded again.

"Go get your stuff ready and I'll pick you up in half an hour," Harlan said. "It'll be fun times to get to talk about ol' Bunny."

Car thanked him, slipped his laptop into the briefcase and left. When Doris returned from the kitchen and saw only Harlan there, she sighed.

"Thought I told you not to go running off the customers."

"I'll have you know I'm picking him up in half an hour to take him to the old Carmichael house," Harlan said. "Ain't every day we get to meet new people from around here."

"Just go easy on him, Harlan. We don't want to scare him off."

"Just showing the boy some hospitality, Doris," he said. He winked at her. "And maybe I ain't the only one?"

She rolled her eyes. But he saw her blush and knew he'd struck a nerve.

"I'm sorry," he said. It was a genuine apology. If anyone deserved a little joy, it was Doris.

"So, you like this guy."

She didn't take the bait and changed the subject. "What are the doctors saying? You cured?"

"Well, they don't call it cured. 'Remission,' they say. But Doc says he thinks he got it all and the chances of it coming back are pretty low."

"Great. So what you're saying is you're going to outlive me and torment me all the way into my grave," she said.

"Yes. That's exactly it, Doris. I got cured just so I could keep you in line and make you bring me more crap decaf."

She topped off his cup from the pot she'd brought to the table with her. "Don't you go getting used to that spot. Soon as you can walk better, I'll make you park out there."

He mock saluted. "Yes, sir."

"I'm glad you're okay, Harlan. Even if you are a pain in my ass."

Chapter Forty–One

Doris had been almost asleep when her cell phone rang. It was Car, asking if she could come to the motel. He had a gift he wanted to give her before he left town the following morning. Now, standing at the door of his motel room, Doris felt more ridiculous than ever before. She did not know what she expected or even should expect. After all, Car was a man of the world, a filmmaker. What was she? A career waitress in a one-stoplight town. Before she could turn and rush back to her house, the door opened and there he was.

"I thought I heard a car. How long were you standing here?"

She stepped past him and into the room. "Longer than I'd like to admit."

She tossed her purse onto the dresser and sat down on the foot of the bed. Rooms at the motel were small, even by motel standards. Car's room was on the older of the two wings. Walnut paneling and syrup-colored carpet seemed to swallow up the meager light cast by the bedside lamp. The brass-and-glass fixture over the window cast a pool of light onto the small table. The first time she had come here the table was overflowing with papers and computer disks. Tonight, though, everything was organized into neat stacks of colored folders. The khaki duffle bag was still open, its top flap propped against the mirror.

As she had done on her previous visit to this room, she paused and studied the photographs. The pictures were secured with a single sheet of plastic laminate to the canvas lining of the bag. It was a kind of improvised shrine to his family and Doris wondered in how many exotic locales Car had opened this very bag and smiled, traveling for work but still managing to keep his family close.

She saw reflected in the mirror over the dresser his laptop, open on the bed, and noticed several jungle scenes open in tiny video windows.

"New movie?"

"Yes. I was working on the Final Cut for a new documentary about Borneo," he said. "I send you a copy when we are finished, yes? I apologize for the poor wrapping," he said. "But I wanted you to have this."

He handed her a small package, neatly wrapped in plain copy paper. She tugged at a corner until the tape gave way. Running her finger along the back, she carefully slipped the paper off the package and removed a DVD case. Inside, she saw her reflection on the face of a disk.

"You finished it already?"

"I wanted to give it to you first," he said.

She looked for a DVD player. He shook his head. "No. Watch it at home. Tonight, we can talk. Yes?"

She couldn't respond. If she opened her mouth, she was afraid she would start to cry. Car sat down beside her. "Doris, have I offended you?"

"No, not at all. It's just, well silly, really. This is the first gift I've gotten from a man in a long, long time."

He pulled her into the crook of his arm and rested her head on his shoulder. "One day, you come to see me in Holland. I have a brother and he will give you lots of gifts."

She blotted tears from her eyes. "Yeah. Right."

"Doris, why do you talk like this? You will come see me one day and I will show you my home as you showed me yours."

"You've been all over the world. There are still parts of this county I haven't seen, Car. You're a documentary filmmaker. I'm a waitress. And people my age don't go making trips like that. People would say I'd lost it."

He lifted her head up. "I tell you a secret. My ma, she always wanted to come back but was afraid of what people say. But Doris is not afraid. You are fearless. I will make you a deal."

"What's that?"

"You come one day, we take you to dinner. Someone will bring you your food for a change. Okay?" He waited for her to agree before he stood and pulled her to her feet. "Now, we walk. This room is depressing."

They followed the gravel path beside the motel down to the fishing pond at the back of the property. There was no moon, so the sky was filled with stars. He stopped and pointed up.

"Where I live, you cannot see the stars. There is too much interference from the lights."

She followed his gaze to the sky. "You like stars?"

"I travel and I see them. I think, maybe, if I were not a documentarian, I might become astronomer. Instead of watching animals, I would watch stars," Car said.

Doris was still thinking about the stars three days later as she moved about the restaurant and ignored the empty stool by the register. Getting on with life meant moving forward. For Doris, that meant it was time to refill Harlan's coffee cup.

He didn't look up from the paper as she poured. "So your boy left town?"

"He wasn't my boy," she said.

"Well, you sure seemed taken by him. Maybe you'll keep in touch?"

Doris didn't answer. She moved on to the Johnson brothers at the next booth. Car's address, phone number and e-mail were safely secured under a magnet on her refrigerator. Whether or not she would ever write or call was a different matter, and it was a matter that was no concern of Harlan's. Throughout the morning, each time the bells rang against the door, she looked up with the hope that the departing customer was Harlan. He understood how she felt about Car and just his knowing was growing into a suffocating pressure. He stayed, though, through lunch, until the last of the plates were cleared away.

When they were at last alone, he called her over. "Have a seat."

"Harlan, I'm–"

"Sit down, please, Doris. I just want to talk."

She wanted to argue but lacked the energy. It had been a long day already and she was due for a tutoring session with Téo within the half hour. "Talk quick. I got things to do."

He stared past her, out into the parking lot. "Going through what I have makes a person think about a lot of things. Things I ain't necessarily thought about before."

"Harlan, what are you on about?"

"Well, take for instance my place. We live twenty miles from the nearest gas station. What would Reenie do if something happened to me?" Harlan said. He stopped, as if waiting for her to answer.

"What's this got to do with me?"

"Not much, at least not yet I don't think. It's just something I've been turning over in my head."

He took a swig of coffee and shuddered. "Gone cold."

She moved to stand but he stopped her. "Let it sit. Stay."

"Harlan, I'm busy–"

"Listen. What would you do if you didn't have your house?"

She glared at him, unsure of where he was headed. Regardless of the direction, she knew she did not like whatever was about to come next.

"Doris, what I'm trying to say is, I think you should sell me your house."

She bolted up. Her cheeks were red and her pulse pounding. "Harlan–"

"Doris, I ain't saying give it to me, damn it. You know very well you ain't ever going to be able to come up with the money to fix it. And even if you did. Why? What for?"

She wanted to slap him. Harlan knew how hard she had fought to keep that house in the family. Paying off the two mortgages her granddaddy left had all but killed her mama. Now, in swoops Harlan Cotton to save the day.

"Harlan–"

"Doris, stop. For just a second, doll. And hear me out."

She was telling her feet to run, but they had grown roots and wouldn't budge. Some part of her brain was hell bent on hearing out the stupidity coming out of Harlan's mouth. He had thought it all out in the past few days, he told her. He would pay full value, even though it would need a lot of work. The Barros man would do the work for him. Then he could move Noreen into town. That way, if something happened, she wouldn't be too far from friends and family. Doris would be free to go wherever she wanted.

"And you'd have enough money to do it up right," he said. "I can afford it. I got the money. Let me do this for you."

With this last sentence, she looked down at him. He truly thought buying her house would be doing her some grand favor, that he could just write a check and make her life magically better. At last, her feet gave way and she stormed out the door. She heard the door open and turned to find him limping across the parking lot after her.

"Doris, stop!" he called. She ignored him.

She found her keys in her purse and was inside the car, the door shut, by the time he reached her.

"Doris, I'm sorry," he said. "I just thought you'd–"

"That's always been your problem, Harlan. You just thought! Well maybe you should stop that sometime," she said through the window. She turned the key over and revved the engine. He stepped back just in time for her to slam the car into drive and lay rubber onto the highway. Not only had Harlan ruined her day, she was now ten minutes late to tutoring with Téo.

Chapter Forty–Two

Doris arrived at Joe's house just as the last vestiges of real daylight crept behind the tree line at the edge of the pasture. Vítor's truck was not in the garage and the house was dark, save a single light over the kitchen window. She checked her watch and decided she would wait. Grabbing a magazine from the back seat, she made a nest on the porch swing and began to read an article about sensible shoes. She was just about to the point where she would learn, once and for all the writer promised, which shoe was perfect for her, when in the distance she heard a whistle.

Silhouetted against the horizon, near the road, a man was standing next to a horse.

"Doris?" the man called out.

"Ted, is that you?" she asked, though his voice had confirmed it enough. "What are you doing out this far this time of day?"

"Just keeping an eye on the place," he said as he approached. He hopped down out of the saddle and pulled off his gloves. "What are you doing out here?"

"Not that it's any of your business, but I came to see Téo."

"Well they ain't here," Ted said. He spat a plug of tobacco onto the ground.

"I can see that, Ted. I don't suppose you know where he is?"

He kicked dirt over the wad with the toe of his boot. "Well, just so happens I do."

She was starting to lose patience. "I ain't gonna beg you to–"

"He's gone into town to clean out the Creedmore Building," Ted said. His voice was flat, absent any hint of confrontation. For a second, she thought she detected the tiniest hint of remorse but dismissed it. She also recognized something else.

"You know where Joe went, don't you?"

Ted just shrugged. "I haven't got a clue. He turned up at the house two days before he left, said maybe it was time to move on. Something about having stayed too long and not knowing when it was time to get out."

Doris leaned back against the car, stared down at her feet. It shouldn't have been a surprise, really. After all, Joe's heart never was in Cranston and he had always been the one guy everyone expected to leave town. Despite Joe's never having even hinted at the desire to travel, Doris always got the idea that his land–his aunt's land–had been a boat anchor, tying him to the land, to the town against his will. She looked up at the house, impeccable and crisp and white, and sighed.

Ted filled in the silence. "When Joe was over, he said he'd leave if he ever had the opportunity. I could tell something wasn't quite right, but I just let him talk. He rambled on about Casey, about Carly, about his aunt. Said he never got a chance to see the world. I said it wasn't too late. It isn't like Joe was an old man or anything. Gosh, he's a couple years younger than me and Marge and I manage to get around, I told him. Said he still could. That's when he asked me."

She had expected him to continue, but Ted had stopped abruptly. She looked up, figuring he was just waiting for her to ask, but he was staring out towards the sunset, and something in his face told her this was a different Ted than she was used to seeing.

"Ted?"

He flinched.

"Huh, Doris?"

"You said he asked you something. What did he ask you?"

"He asked me if I'd buy the Creedmore Building and the half of his acreage here that butts up to our place. Made me an offer so good I had to double it just to make myself not feel guilty. Traveling money, he called it."

"Why only half?"

He laughed.

"That's the damnedest part of the whole deal. I asked him that same question and you know what he told me? Said it wasn't his anymore."

"I don't understand."

"Vítor Barros. And that son of his. They're going to live here. Joe gave it to them."

She wanted to cry, but didn't. Instead, from somewhere deep inside, she began to laugh, unable to stop herself. Her sides were hurting and she was having trouble breathing. She bent over, her head between her legs, trying to force air into her lungs.

Ted shook her shoulder. "What the hell's so funny?"

She waved him off. "You don't get it, do you?" She looked into his face, all quizzical and baffled, and hoped she saw some hint of recognition. But where she hoped to find a glimmer of a clue forming, she found only the blank, absent stare of someone completely confused.

"You don't get it and you never will. Not you, not Harlan. Certainly not Harlan."

She stuck out her hand, almost formally. "It's been nice knowing you, Ted Bartley."

"Excuse me?"

"I'm saying good bye, you jackass. Shake my hand."

He took her hand, noncommittally shook it, and held it for a second. Finally, it clicked. "Son of a bitch. You too."

She took one last look at Joe's empty house and nodded. "Yep, Ted. I guess so. You'll keep an eye on Jimmy for me?"

"You people beat all I've ever seen," Ted said. "Whole world right here and going to go running off to what? To find yourselves?"

"Something like that," she said. She climbed into the car, rolled down all four windows and opened the sunroof. "I'd say see you around, Ted, but I don't think I will."

As she started to back the car down the drive, she leaned out the window. "Give Margie my best!"

She steered the car out onto the highway and, finally, let the weight of her decision sink in. She was leaving home. No, that wasn't right. She was leaving Cranston and that shell of a house. She was leaving the Café and an endless parade of "Would you like fries with that?" in exchange for so many unknowns that any picture of tomorrow she conjured looked so unrecognizable she could not make it her own.

A moment of panic swept over her.

Doris knew exactly two people outside of Cranston. Carly was settled into her new life at the university and Car would be meeting his family sometime today for their trip through the Southwest. Not a good batch of options for starting over, she knew.

Doris Greely had spent all her days in the ten square miles that accounted for Cranston and she was in her car, racing up Macomb Road toward some vast unknown future. In Cranston, she was a Greely. The last of them, in fact. That meant something here.

She was stupid, crazy even, for thinking she could pull it off. She kicked herself for believing it was possible. After all, she had what, three or four thousand in her bank account? It might take months to sell the house to Harlan. How would she live until then? Pay her bills? She saw the highway and the stop sign and brought the car to a halt.

She glanced into her purse and saw she had missed three calls, all from Jimmy. No doubt telling her how much trouble she was in while somehow managing to beg her to be at work on time tomorrow.

She turned her blinker on, signaling to the nonexistent traffic behind her that she would turn left. It was still early enough that she'd catch him in time to tell him yes, she'd be at work tomorrow morning.

She nervously drummed her fingers on the steering wheel. Yet she could not bring herself to press the accelerator and instead turned off the blinker. Before her, taunting her, the road sign was clear. Cranston and Harlan and the boys and the diner, two miles to the left. To the right, Waco ninety miles, then Austin and beyond that...?

"Sorry Jimmy," she said aloud.

Doris let her foot slip from the brake and felt the car ease forward and she began to cut the wheel. She closed her eyes and held her breath.

The End

Acknowledgements and Notes on the Second Edition

It isn't often a writer gets to say "Thank You" twice in the same text. Yet, when presented with that opportunity more than four years after The Patriot Joe Morton first appeared in print, I looked back over who made this book possible, what went into the words on this page, and I realize again the touch of insanity it takes for a writer to sit down and write a novel. In spite of the author's work, a book is as much a collaborative effort as a well-performed symphony. The composer pens the music and, occasionally, conducts its premier. More times than not, though, someone else conducts—a new artist. And in no case can a composer perform all parts of a symphony himself. There are dozens of musicians—flutists, trombonists, percussionists, even several individuals devoted to the maligned French horn. A book is quite the same, and in this respect, we pause to say thank you to those other artists who helped make this little book a reality.

First, I send my gratitude and appreciation to Doug and Heather at Arctic Wolf Publishing, who first decided to take a chance on one of my stories back in 2010. The folly of writing a novel is trumped only by the Sisyphean task of running a small press. Without small presses, too many worthwhile stories would go unread. I've been privileged now to have worked closely with two such endeavors, and Miika Hannila at Creativia is unmatched in professionalism and courtesy.

I must also thank above others my good friend, Martha Brown, from whose fertile imagination sprang the central device of this story. Without that car ride almost a decade ago, this story would have remained consigned to the ether, waiting to be discovered by some other writer.

There is no way I could have persevered without the prodding, guidance and encouragement of my own holy trinity: Carolyn Meinel, Marcy Hall and Ann Bloxom Smith. To Carolyn, I say thank you for giving me the motivation to keep my chin up through the dark times and the kudos when it's clicking. It is you who made sure that Harlan had a heart and Doris became a woman. Marcy, without your eagle eye, there's no telling what might have happened between the breach and the breech. And to Ann, the best editor a writer could ever hope for, there are not words. Every writer should be so lucky to be able to avail themselves of the talents of the three of you.

This book is not about finding truth. It's not about changing your mind any more than it is about changing the world. It's a story that I hope entertained you through these scant few pages. If you found truth, if you found some moral or some lesson, then consider it a bonus. For that was certainly not my intent.

When I first sat down to write Joe Morton's story, the United States was again in the grip of an unpopular war, a war that many of us felt we had won more than nine years earlier. We questioned why our troops were still engaged and dying in a battle on sands of deserts we would never visit. All the while, the winds of change were blowing and a new president had promised to remove us from those fields of battle. We're still there, for what it's worth. Whether you agree with war, this war or any war, or find the very notion of war morally repugnant, please take just a moment and thank the men and women who wear the uniform. While I do not for a moment believe my freedom to write this book is a gift paid for by the military, I am nevertheless quite thankful that the Army, the Air Force, the Navy and the Marines wake up each morning, report for duty, and defend this great nation. For this, they are patriots all.

Michael DeVault
Monroe, Louisiana
May 19, 2014